"I've grown up. I don't flit from thing to thing like I did in high school," Angelina said.

Tyler nodded, his eyes measuring her.

"You can trust me," she whispered. "I know what my feelings are. They're not going to go away tomorrow because some new and exciting thing happens."

Angelina watched the emotions roll across Tyler's face. His disbelief. His uncertainty. Followed by something she thought was hope. And then it was all gone. There wasn't a flicker of anything left.

"You don't believe me," she said, her voice flat.

He swallowed and looked at her. "No, I think maybe I do believe you."

He didn't look very certain about it, though, and Angelina blinked back the dampness in her eyes. "I'll prove it to you. Wait and see. I'm a changed person."

"But I'm not," he said.

She could not argue with that. Only God could change the heart of a man. She knew without asking that there would be no more confiding in each other tonight.

Grant me patience, Lord, she prayed silently. *Help Tyler to see he needs to change, too.*

Books by Janet Tronstad

Love Inspired

JANET TRONSTAD

currently lives in Pasadena, California, but she grew up on a farm in central Montana so she knows how dusty the back roads can be in those rural areas. She's driven down many of them, although not in a red convertible as Angelina Brighton does in this book. Maybe someday. In the meantime, she drives a modest car and enjoys travel, plays and spending time with friends and family.

Wildflower Bride in Dry Creek

Janet Tronstad

Love Inspired

Recycling programs
for this product may
not exist in your area.

™ LOVE INSPIRED BOOKS

ISBN-13: 978-0-373-87753-9

WILDFLOWER BRIDE IN DRY CREEK

www.LoveInspiredBooks.com

Printed in U.S.A.

Honor thy father and thy mother:
that thy days may be long upon the land
which the Lord thy God giveth thee.
—*Exodus* 20:12

I dedicate this book to my buddies in the
East Valley Authors group, my local chapter within
the Romance Writers of America organization.
The writers in this Azusa, California, group are
unfailingly encouraging and persistent. Each
year we have an "Outwrite Janet" contest and
everyone tries to get down more words than I do
in the month. One year a team of two even won
the challenge, which delighted me. To call out just
some of their names—there's Beth, Charity, Alison,
Shannon, Laura, Julie, Debra, Joy, Riccarla, Carol,
Roberta, Mary, Maria, Erin, Sherry and Marlene.

Chapter One

Tyler Stone loosened his grip on the steering wheel and eased his pickup to a stop at the edge of the small town of Dry Creek, Montana. He would never call this place home again and yet, here he was, looking down the street with a longing he hadn't expected. All of the old clapboard houses stood silent, their cement steps leading to doors that were firmly closed against the July heat.

"Nothing has changed," Tyler muttered to himself as he kept staring at the empty street.

It seemed impossible that the betrayal his family had experienced in this town hadn't left some outward mark on the buildings themselves. But none of the windows were boarded up. Not one house was deserted. Ten years ago, reporters had been knocking on the doors of all the buildings, demanding to know what kind of a woman Tyler's mother had been that she could kill her husband. The media had little compassion as she went on trial for her life, and Tyler wished he knew which of these doors had opened to spill the gossip about the Stone family.

His father's drunken abuse, their general unhappiness, even the time their electricity had been turned off for lack of payment had all made it into the news.

Suddenly, Tyler saw a flash of movement out of his left eye. A tremor raced through his hands until he realized it was only the reflection of the afternoon sun on his windshield.

"Easy now," he said to himself as he wiped his hands on his jeans. He didn't have time to worry about which neighbor had done what in the past. He had enough problems in the present. He had been hired to escort Angelina Brighton back to her home in Boston. If he couldn't convince her to go, he'd be out of a job. And not a newspaper in the world would even care.

This wasn't the first time he had been hired to babysit Angelina. She had been his last assignment with Brighton Security, the one right before he went into the military. Her father had received some kidnapping threats regarding her so Tyler had been assigned to serve as one of her bodyguards during her senior year of high school. At nineteen years old, he'd been chosen for the job because he could blend in with the other students and stay close to Angelina. All he was supposed to do in a bad situation was to summon the older Brighton guards who were there in the distance. No one had expected him to stop the kidnapping, identify a stalker and then dance with Angelina at the prom after her date waltzed off with another girl.

He remembered her father had barely blinked an eye at the kidnapping attempt, but he'd almost fired Tyler over the dance. Mr. Brighton had coldly informed Tyler that he had higher aspirations for his only child than for her to marry some half-breed Native American boy with criminal blood flowing through his veins. Tyler didn't mind what the man said about his heritage; he had always been proud that he looked like his Cherokee ancestors and nothing much could change that.

But he never talked about his mother or the fact that she was in prison for murdering his father. The shame of that burned deep inside him because, when all was said and done, Tyler knew the tragedy had somehow been his fault. He had been twelve years old, which in the Cherokee world was grown enough to be considered a man. But he hadn't had the nerve to go into the barn that awful day when he overheard his father throwing things and cursing his name. The man had a violent temper, and Tyler still had the bruises from his last beating. So he ran away, back to the house, where he hid. He never knew what his mother had said in response to his father or how long they argued or how she happened to strike that fatal blow. All Tyler knew was if he had gone inside that barn, things would have ended differently.

He glanced down at the photo of Angelina that he had taped to his dashboard. He hadn't asked for the photo, but her father, his boss, had given it to him anyway. Blonde, blue-eyed and petite, Angelina looked like a fashion doll at twenty-three years old. Tyler was only a year older than her, but he felt like he had been dragged through the bottom mud long enough to be many times her age. Of course, being in the military could do that to a man, especially when he was a special ops guy trying to infiltrate the Pashtun tribal region with only his wits for backup.

Just then a faint humming sound made Tyler look up into his rearview mirror. A car was approaching from behind. His left arm was still healing so he reached over with his right hand to roll up the window on his pickup, hoping whoever it was would drive by. Then the car got closer, and he saw it was a shiny red convertible—one that he recognized all too well.

Angelina was coming into town with the top down on her sports car and her long blond hair blowing in the wind. *She always did live with gusto,* he thought as he grinned for the first time in months.

When the convertible sped past, he realized Angelina was driving much too fast. What did she think she was doing? He knew she never took the slow way anywhere, but she had to live long enough to make it back to Boston or there would be no paycheck for him.

Tyler turned the key in his ignition. He had barely pulled back onto the road when he saw a sheriff's car come out from behind the café.

Good, he thought. The law was going to deal with her.

Just then the convertible screeched to a halt and started to back up at the same speed it had gone forward. Tyler had no choice but to pull off the road again. Only Angelina would try to outrun a lawman by putting her car in Reverse. Life was too precious to drive like a maniac and someone needed to tell Angelina that, he told himself. By the time she came parallel to him, the convertible screeched again as she put on the brakes.

Before it seemed possible, Angelina had flung open her door. The dust was still settling when she stepped out of her car. Then she stood up, turned and leaned forward, bracing her hands against the side of her convertible.

"Where'd you get that pickup?" she demanded.

Of all the things he'd expected her to say, that wasn't one of them. He knew she couldn't see him clearly enough to recognize him. She confirmed that when she put up one of her hands to shade her eyes from the sun as she squinted in his direction.

"I'd know that pickup anywhere," she continued, her voice still strong but sounding less sure of herself. "Not many old black pickups have a dent on one side and an Indian head bumper sticker like that on the other."

The bumper sticker, a chief in full headdress, was one of the few things Tyler had taken with him when he left the family ranch. He had been determined to be a warrior after that day by the barn. Longing to be self-sufficient and strong, he pledged not to fear anyone, or need them either. If he'd taken his beating like a man, no one would have died and his mother would be home in her kitchen baking pies instead of sitting in some prison.

Tyler opened his mouth to answer, but no words came out. He couldn't do much more than breathe. He'd forgotten how vibrant Angelina was when she was stirred up. Her blond hair looked like spun gold and it floated around her as she started marching around the car on her way toward his pickup.

"That's Tyler Stone's pickup." She rounded the side of her convertible and pointed right at him. "He left it at my father's place and no one has permission to drive it. No one."

She was fearless.

Tyler finally forced his pulse to slow down. All he owned was this old pickup truck and maybe some interest in his family's deserted ranch. His modest prospects were the main reason her father had forbid him to show any interest in her. And, on that one point, Tyler had agreed. He was poor and he knew what it was to do without. He could never ask Angelina to give up her trust fund money and he couldn't accept any of it either. A man had to have some pride. No, they had no choice but to part at the end of her senior year.

"It's me," he managed to say.

Her face had gone paler than Tyler liked, but he supposed he had no right to expect her to be happy to see him. She'd called him her jailer more than once. He was used to hauling her out of trouble. He should have told Brighton Security to send someone else.

"But you're supposed to be dead!" she said with shock in her voice.

"It was a misunderstanding," Tyler said as he scrambled to make sense of what had happened. "I wasn't really dead. The notification was a mistake."

He remembered how he had managed to get the three Pashtun children to safety before the bomb exploded, but he was left standing too close. He ended up with a big red burn along his right side and a piece of metal in his knee that slowed him down considerably. His left arm suffered some damage and he couldn't easily make a fist on that hand. After the explosion, the parents of those children had carried him to a hospital where he'd lain semiconscious and unidentified for weeks. He'd been gone so long that, when the villagers said he'd been killed in the bomb blast, his unit had given him up for dead. The notification was supposed to say Missing in Action, but somehow things had gotten confused.

"And you never thought to tell me you were still alive?" Angelina exclaimed, her sapphire-blue eyes flashing at him.

"I—ah—" He hadn't thought she would have cared.

Tyler moved his head, leaning farther out the window, hoping it would ease the situation if she could see him better. That's when the brim of his Stetson hit the edge of the open window and was knocked off his head. He watched the cream-colored hat fall straight down into the dirt. Without his hat, the sunlight hit his face full strength.

"You really are Tyler Stone." Angelina's lips pursed together and she shook her head. Then she did the most amazing thing. She calmly walked over to where his hat sat on the ground, bent down and picked it up, then brushed it off and offered it to him.

"You'll need this," she said, her words clipped.

The Angelina he remembered was never that matter-of-fact and controlled.

"I'm sorry," he managed to say. "I should have thought to—to—"

He really wasn't sure what he could have done. "You know, I never even had your phone number. How did you expect me to get you the news anyway?"

He certainly couldn't pass the word through her father, and she must have known that.

"You could have figured it out," she snapped back. "Before I made a fool of myself."

"You're no fool," he protested automatically.

He never guessed she had known about the death notification from the military. Tyler had asked to list her father's firm on his papers as next of kin because he didn't want to disturb his mother in prison. The man had reluctantly agreed. That's why Mr. Brighton had known to meet Tyler's plane when he got back from Afghanistan. He never thought anyone but the office staff had ever known or cared about the notification.

Tyler reached out to retrieve his hat from Angelina, but had completely forgotten about his left hand. So when he went to grip the hat, he couldn't grab hold of the brim. Before he could stop it, the Stetson floated to the ground again.

"Oh." He heard a gasp and looked up.

"Why, you're hurt," she whispered, her voice thick with pity. All of the color rushed back into her face.

Tyler looked down at his hand. The nerves had been damaged and the skin was still puckered red from the burn. His whole hand had a tendency to swell in the

heat and look puffy. He planned to start physical therapy after he got Angelina back home.

"I'm fine," he said because he didn't know what else
to say.

By now, the sheriff's car had pulled up on the other
side of Angelina's convertible. As the man in the patrol car stepped closer, Tyler realized it was Sheriff Carl
Wall. He looked just the same. Then Tyler noticed the
sheriff held the leash of a brown dog that had a pink
ribbon draped around its neck. At least that was something new. The lawman hadn't been in charge of animal
control duty before.

The canine whimpered a little in the silence. Tyler
wondered if the dog sensed the tension.

If there was one person Tyler had never wanted to
see again it was Sheriff Wall. The last time Tyler had
set eyes on him had been a cold winter day. The sheriff
had come out to the Stone ranch and helped carry his
father's murdered body out of the barn. Then he had
turned right around and arrested Tyler's mother.

"I heard rumors you were in the military," the lawman finally said, rocking back on his heels. "Special
Ops, I thought it was. Run into problems?"

"Nothing I couldn't handle." Tyler didn't want sympathy from the sheriff or Angelina so he unlatched the
door to his pickup and started to open it. "And I got out
of the service a week ago."

The door of Tyler's pickup swung wide. When he
had room, he stepped to the ground and reached out

with his right hand to pick up his hat. He brushed the Stetson against the sides of his jeans.

Tyler couldn't stop his left hand from trembling.

Just then the dog walked over to smell Tyler's boots.

"Come back here, Prince," the sheriff commanded with a tug on the animal's leash.

The dog just raised its head and stared at the lawman.

"What kind of name is Prince for a dog like this anyway?" Tyler asked as he bent down to scratch the canine behind its ears. He was at a loss as to what to say to Angelina, but he didn't want her to leave either. "Looks more like a mutt to me."

"It's a stray," the sheriff replied with a shrug.

"Prince is *my* dog now," Angelina interrupted them both as she took a step closer. "And I thought he needed a boost to his self-esteem after being on his own so I named him Prince Charming."

"I shortened it to Prince," the sheriff hastened to add.

"So what did Prince do to earn a ride in the county car?" Tyler asked, letting go of the dog and standing up.

"Prince ran away," Angelina answered, her voice wavering a little. "The sheriff called me to come get him."

Tyler had heard that little hitch in her voice before and he knew what it meant. Without thinking, he did what he always did. He turned to pat her shoulder with his right arm. Unfortunately, he wasn't as smooth with his movements as he used to be and somehow the pat turned into a hug and, before he knew it, Angelina was sobbing against his shirt and he had his arm around her like he had the right. That's when he forgot himself and kissed the top of her head, right where she parted her golden hair. She smelled of coconut and sunshine so he breathed deep. He looked up to see the sheriff watching.

Tyler glared at the man.

"Hey." The lawman held up his hands in surrender. "I never come between—" He paused and thought a moment. "What are you two anyway? Boyfriend and girlfriend?"

Angelina gasped and looked up. "Certainly not."

Her cheeks flamed.

"She was my employer," Tyler said. "The daughter of my employer, I mean."

"He saved my life," Angelina added and burst into a whole new set of tears. "And now—I've killed him."

She stepped away from him at that.

"What?" Tyler blinked. He knew Angelina didn't always describe exactly what she meant. That was part of her charm. But she made a pretty bold statement for an unarmed woman who couldn't even see clear enough through her tears to do any damage to a fly.

He looked to her for further explanation and all she did was hiccup.

"I think she means there's an event planned in your honor for this evening," the sheriff finally said with a grin. "I hadn't thought I'd go, but I just might show up. Should prove interesting."

"I was making those little quiches," Angelina added in a soft voice. She looked up at him and her eyes shimmered. "The tiny ones, you know—and homemade, not the frozen kind. They're lots of work. And some sausage-stuffed mushrooms, too. That's why Prince got away. I couldn't cook and watch him at the same time." Her eyes brightened. "I've been the relief cook for the Elkton ranch for a month now. It'll be another month until the regular cook comes back. The ranch has ovens big enough for the appetizers so I volunteered to make them there."

"You have a job?" He was dumbfounded. Tyler had thought her father must be wrong when he told him that. With her trust fund, Angelina had enough money to live like a princess. *"Why?"*

"Everyone needs to contribute to the world," she said, squaring her shoulders.

Tyler lifted his eyebrow. The Angelina he remembered had never worried about the good of the world.

"Jesus didn't sit around doing nothing," she added, as if he hadn't heard her the first time.

"You mean you cook for the church parties?" Tyler asked, figuring that must be her latest passion. Maybe she made appetizers and folded napkins and offered up some kind of a prayer for a ladies tea or something. "The ranch cook has to feed the cowboys and, when they've been working, they eat like a pack of wild animals. You can't be doing that job."

She didn't respond, but she looked like she was gathering her defenses.

"So, you're giving me a party?" Tyler offered her an olive branch. He was rather fond of those little quiches anyway and wouldn't mind eating a few. He supposed it didn't matter who Angelina was cooking for. It wouldn't last. She'd be on to something new before long.

That's when a realization hit him. "But nobody knew I was coming."

Not that he couldn't appreciate a welcome-home party as much as the next guy, but he hadn't been back in the States long enough to contact anyone but his employer. And nobody in the offices at Brighton Security would give out the location of a guard who was on duty. They'd be fired if they did. If there was a leak, he needed to know about it.

That's when Angelina took a deep breath and brushed her hand over her eyes. She looked at him through her tears. "I can't believe you're really alive."

"I know." It was rather endearing, he thought. Maybe she did have some affection for him, after all.

She shook her head. "No, you don't understand."

She took another deep breath and still hesitated a moment. "I planned a funeral for you tonight."

"A *what?*"

"Well, technically it's not a funeral since we don't have your body." She rushed through the words and then stopped. "At least, we didn't have your body earlier. I guess we do now. But it's a memorial service out at your family's ranch. I have a lot of wildflowers being delivered from Miles City. Some organic ranch by Missoula grows them for sale."

She looked at him, stricken again by some feeling. "I hope you like wildflowers. I never really heard you say what your favorite flower was."

"I don't think I have one," Tyler finally managed to answer.

The sheriff shifted his stance and spoke. "Roses are nice."

"I think I need to sit down," Tyler said and stepped back so he could sit on the sideboard of his pickup. "I'm not sick or anything though. Definitely not dying. Don't order any more flowers."

The sheriff chuckled at that.

The day was certainly hot, Tyler thought to himself as he sat there. He'd faced death a number of times in his life, but he'd never expected to face his funeral. The people of Dry Creek might have gossiped about his mother, but that would be nothing compared to what they would say about him now.

Angelina tried to get a good look at Tyler's face, but his Stetson shaded him as he sat there. He had dark stubble on his chin, so he probably hadn't shaved today. She used to be able to tell what he was thinking by the expression on his face, but she couldn't right now. Suddenly, he lifted his head and his brown eyes flashed at her like he didn't welcome her scrutiny. She felt a rush of embarrassment and turned away so she wasn't staring at the man.

She always did seem to do things wrong when it came to Tyler. He didn't know it, but he'd been her best friend in high school. Of course, after that kidnapping attempt, he was always there, guarding her, so she found herself talking to him more than anyone. She hadn't even complained too much about him being there because she'd never been as scared as when she'd been grabbed and forced into that black van. If Tyler hadn't astonished everyone by pulling out a knife from somewhere and throwing it at a front tire on the vehicle, she could have been taken away and maybe even killed.

"I only planned the memorial service because you saved my life," she finally said. And she had only come to Dry Creek because her best friend, Kelly Norton, had told her that she'd never feel comfortable marrying anyone until she found closure with Tyler. Her father was pressuring her to marry his attorney but she refused to even get to know the man.

"Nice shirt," Angelina added just to hide her nerves. She didn't know how much closure she'd have now that Tyler was alive. He was wearing a Western-style beige shirt with pearl snaps on it and the way it opened at the collar showed the strength of his neck. She was glad Kelly wasn't here to see that or she'd be going on about how handsome and manly Tyler was. Angelina certainly hoped he didn't think she was snooping around his hometown because she still had a crush on him like she had in high school. She never would have come if she thought he'd show up.

"You don't owe me for saving your life," he said finally. "Your father gave me a bonus. I got the engine rebuilt in my pickup with it."

"Well, I didn't go to much trouble," Angelina said, gathering her dignity around her. Fortunately, she hadn't arranged for anyone to sing at the funeral. And the reception afterward was going to be simple even if she expected fifty or so people.

Then she remembered in dismay that she had ordered the gravestone with the custom-carved angel sitting on it. She had figured there should be some marker for Tyler even if he didn't have a final resting place for his bones. Hopefully, the receipt wouldn't be attached when the company delivered it to the ranch. It had been a little expensive, but the salesman had told her it was a memorial forever to a good friend. One of those priceless gestures that are supposed to be important in life.

Now it was just an awkward chunk of marble, nothing but a tribute to her impetuous nature. She couldn't send it back, either, not with the custom features she'd added.

"You couldn't have any event out at the ranch without going to some work," Tyler said as he stood up again. "The house had to be filthy since no one has lived there for over a decade now. It would take a week just to get it in shape."

"Oh," Angelina said and felt the rest of the air go out of her. The gravestone might not be her biggest worry.

The sheriff chuckled again and turned to her. "You best take him out to the ranch so he can see how things are. And won't Mrs. Hargrove be out there rehearsing her prayer?"

"You're having someone *pray* over me?" Tyler asked, clearly alarmed. "I don't have much to do with church and praying, you know."

"Well, you will at your funeral," Angelina snapped.

She was trying to learn patience, but, really, she had meant the service as a kindness to him. "That poor woman prayed for you every day when you were in the military so you can accept a few words at your funeral. She said she'd prayed for you as a boy and she wasn't about to stop when you needed it most."

"She did?" Tyler seemed surprised. "I always liked her. She used to carry lemon drops in her apron pocket for all us kids."

"Well, I want you to know that Mrs. Hargrove kept right on praying for you even when they said you were dead," Angelina continued. "That's why I thought we needed some kind of a service. Lots of people here were praying once they found out you were in the military and they needed closure so they could say goodbye."

Tyler looked stunned. "Why would people pray for me? I never went to the church here—well, except for that one time to Sunday school in the basement. I thought they'd chase me off if I tried to go to the upstairs meetings. My brothers and I were troublemakers. Everyone knew that."

"You were soldier of the month in the prayer chain four times last year," the sheriff said. "They had your picture in the bulletin recently and everything."

Angelina thought the lawman was enjoying this a little too much.

"How did they get a picture of me?" Tyler asked, looking bewildered. "I had just turned thirteen when my brother and I were sent to that state group home. And I don't think anyone took my photo back then anyway."

Sheriff Wall seemed to take delight in pointing to her.

"I gave them the photo," she confessed. Really, it was no big deal. She'd taken pictures of everyone she hung out with in high school. She might have a few more of Tyler than the other students, but that was just because he was always there.

In addition to the closure with Tyler, part of the reason she'd come to Dry Creek was that she remembered him describing the community. This place had always felt like home to her even though she'd never seen it. The church. The small café. The town was like some distant Camelot just waiting for her. Besides, something was going on in her father's house in Boston and she didn't want to stay there. The staff kept whispering and no one would tell her why.

"You go to the church?" Tyler asked her.

"I plan to become a woman of deep faith," she said. She and Mrs. Hargrove were reading the New Testament together. "At least as deep as possible, with God's help."

Tyler looked pained. "You're not becoming a nun or anything are you?"

"Are you working for my father?"

Tyler nodded.

"Then you must know I've become a Christian." She tried to keep the annoyance out of her voice. Being patient was a hard virtue to learn, but she was determined. "I want to know what God wants me to do with my life, not only what my father wants."

"Your father is concerned about you and he's also

worried about your trust fund. Said you'd mentioned giving it away."

"I said I might set up a charitable foundation. Really, my father never paid any attention to me when I was growing up. And now that I'm doing something responsible, he gets all protective."

"He wants what's best for you."

She forced herself to smile and continue. "I have a perfectly ordinary job as a relief cook for the Elkton ranch. Their regular cook is taking care of her ill mother up in Oregon. It was last minute, so they were glad to get someone to fill in for her. I go to church in Dry Creek on Sunday and I read the Bible. That's my life here."

"Well," Tyler said, looking down like there was something interesting about his boots. "Your father said the other reason you're out here is that you're supposed to marry some Daryl guy, but you have cold feet."

"Derrick," she corrected him with more force than was probably necessary. "His name is Derrick Carlson and my feet are perfectly fine."

"So what'd the guy do?" Tyler asked, looking up at her.

The sheriff cleared his throat again. Angelina had forgotten the lawman was there.

"I'll just go take Prince for a walk," the sheriff said.

"You don't need to leave," she told him and then turned back to Tyler. "I have no secrets. Derrick didn't do anything. Nothing at all. I barely know the man. He asked my father for his permission to marry me. I'm afraid my father is suffering from some stress-related problem. I had to try some wedding dress on just to calm him down. And he booked a small church for the ceremony—he actually scheduled it. He gets so agitated when I say I'm not marrying Derrick that I'm afraid he's going to have a heart attack."

"Your father says he's just concerned about your future."

Angelina folded her arms. "He's anxious about something, all right. But it's not me."

"Maybe he just wants you to get to know this Daryl guy."

"It's Derrick. He wears Armani suits and plays golf with my father. I doubt he even wears T-shirts on the weekend."

"Well, that's not a crime," Tyler said. "And he might have a problem with expressing himself."

"He's my father's lawyer. How much of a problem could he have?"

She glanced over at the sheriff. The man was inching away from them.

Angelina turned back to Tyler. She didn't have time to worry about making the sheriff squirm. "I think Derrick needs to be investigated. Who was that guy who used to sneak around and find out things for you anyway? You always made him do that before I could date anyone."

"Clyde?" Tyler looked surprised. "I don't know if he's still in business. And that was high school. It was easy to find out who the jerks were back then. Clyde just hung out in the lunchroom when you weren't around and listened to what they said. He always charged me for his lunch, too, by the way."

"Well, maybe Clyde can investigate Derrick. And have him check into my father, too."

Tyler scowled at her. "Again? I thought you would have learned to trust your father by now."

Angelina willed herself to take a breath. "This isn't like high school. I'm not asking you to investigate my father because I want to get his attention. I really think something's wrong. Maybe Derrick is blackmailing him and that's why my father is insisting I marry the man."

"What would he have on your father?"

"I don't know, "Angelina tried to stay calm. "But even though my father is, well, my father—he could still have this secret life I don't know anything about."

"I thought we settled that. You're not adopted. And your father doesn't have another family hidden away somewhere."

"But you always told me to trust my intuition. And something's wrong."

Tyler closed his eyes. "I meant you should pay attention to your surroundings. If you thought the bush was moving, assume it was."

"Well, the bush is moving—it's my father."

"That's not—" Tyler started and then stopped. "Fine. If it makes you feel better, I'll call Clyde."

"Thank you."

"As I remember, Clyde was taking classes to earn a finance degree," Tyler said. "Claimed he wanted to end up on Wall Street. He's probably wearing an Armani suit himself now."

"We've all changed." She hadn't realized how much she'd missed Tyler. She wondered if he'd stay in touch with her this time. After high school, he had just ridden off into the sunset without a look back to see if she was standing there watching him leave.

"And even if we give Clyde a free lunch, he'll want to be paid regular, too," Tyler said.

Angelina nodded. "You know I have money."

He grunted at that. "You're an heiress. I know."

"That's not who I am," she snapped back.

Then she realized she was a working woman now. And she was supposed to have the evening meal on the table by five-thirty in the Elkton bunkhouse. She had a nice beef stew in the oven and had told the ranch hands to be punctual because Tyler's memorial service was scheduled for seven-thirty. She had insisted they all go, and the foreman had backed her up. When the cowboys hesitated, she had promised them biscuits with honey butter. She didn't know what the foreman had offered them.

Whatever it was though they would probably still want their biscuits. But before she could make any, there was something else she needed to do.

"I need to go out to your ranch," she told Tyler. She had to explain things to his family before she could think of feeding the ranch hands. "You may as well ride with me."

"In that?" Tyler looked at her convertible like it was

a leaky tub she was planning to set afloat in a raging flood. "That thing isn't made for these country roads. And your driving isn't—"

"Fine," she interrupted him. Why had she decided to have a funeral for the one man who felt free to criticize her? Maybe he only spoke his mind so freely because they were friends. But right now she didn't have time to argue. "I'll ride with you then."

She walked over and pushed the button that put up the roof on her car.

"Don't forget Prince here," the sheriff said as he let go of the dog's leash.

"He rides in the back," Tyler said.

"But he could fall out," Angelina protested as she pushed another button to roll up her windows.

"Not at the speed I drive these roads," Tyler said. "Only fools go fast on gravel roads. It makes too much dust and ruins your shocks."

With that he turned his back on her and headed toward his pickup. Prince, the traitor, followed right along with him, his leash and the ribbon she'd put on him this morning, trailing behind.

She wished she could just refuse to ride with Tyler, she thought as she hurried after them. But she needed to prepare him. She really hadn't intended to meddle in his life, she assured herself as she walked to the other side of his pickup. Of course, it couldn't be seen as interfering since she'd thought he was dead.

Tyler opened the passenger door for her and she started to climb into the vehicle. He was reasonable.

Maybe he would even see the gravestone with the angel as a compliment. It's not like she had gotten the one with the inset photograph on it, she reminded herself. Now, that would have been extravagant.

She sat down on the seat in the cab. And that's when she saw the photo.

"You've got my picture," she said, pointing to it. "Right there."

She hated that picture. Her father's secretary had taken the shot, and Angelina thought it made her look like a porcelain doll. No one needed a wedding dress with that much netting. But when she complained, her father had merely sent the garment back for adjustments.

"Ah—" Tyler stopped with his hand on the door. "It was for identification purposes."

"You needed a picture to identify me! We spent my whole senior year together."

"Well, of course, I know what you look like," Tyler said as he put his right hand up and ran his fingers through his hair. She remembered that gesture. It meant he didn't want to admit something.

"Then why did you have the picture?" she asked, some of her pride soothed.

"I was trying to figure out why you were marrying that Daryl guy."

"Derrick," she corrected him automatically. "His name is *Derrick*. And I'm not marrying him."

"Your father said the wedding was all set and is just postponed."

"There is no wedding."

"I have a feeling that will change," Tyler said gloomily and with that he shut her door.

She watched him walk around the pickup toward his own door. Strangely enough, she kind of liked that he was curious about her and Derrick. She had confided in Tyler when she was in high school, but that was a long time ago. She wondered if he might be just a little bit jealous.

The truth was she didn't have good radar when it came to men. Mrs. Hargrove was helping her correct that and, when she had gotten to know the older woman, Angelina could see that Mrs. Hargrove and her husband were deeply in love with each other and with God. They had given her hope that she might find someone special like that, too, someday.

All of her life Angelina had felt like she was on the outskirts of something warm and cozy because she was not important to anyone's happiness. Maybe if her mother hadn't died when she was young, she would have more of a sense of being part of a family. But it had just been her and her father for as long as she could remember and he had been preoccupied with building his empire. What he had was never enough for him.

Tyler opened his door and climbed into the driver's seat of the pickup.

Of course, Tyler never needed anyone or anything but himself, either.

Her big problem, she told herself still looking at him out of the corner of her eye, was that she always fell for the bad boys. She liked to believe one of them would draw her so close that his life would be empty without her. Unfortunately, good girls with trust funds should never go for the bad boys. Her father hadn't given her much advice, or attention, over the years, but he had drilled that one lesson into her teenage head.

She wasn't sure, but she thought her father had Tyler in mind when he gave her that lecture.

Of course, she doubted Mrs. Hargrove would think Tyler was the one for her, either. It'd be hard for him to claim he was a godly man and that was number one on the older woman's qualities for a husband.

"Don't you ever pray?" she asked him now, her voice quiet.

Tyler looked at her and shook his head.

Well, she knew that, she told herself. There was no need for disappointment. She just needed to press forward with the memorial tonight. Maybe that would help her say a final goodbye to Tyler.

Chapter Two

Tyler kept his eyes on the road as he drove. The afternoon sun was low in the sky, but it was behind him so he could see clearly without squinting. His window was down a little and the faint smell of sage drifted in. He was trying to keep things between him and Angelina in perspective. Her tears hadn't been for him personally. It had been unsettling for her to see someone she thought was dead, but that would pass.

Her feelings had always been delicate.

Besides, her father was right to warn him away from her. If he ever married, Tyler told himself he should marry someone who knew what it was like to survive with little money. Someone who'd grown up in the country like he had. He might still think about Angelina, but that was probably just because that year guarding her had been the happiest one of his life. He hadn't had many friends in his life and no one bubbled over with happiness like she did.

He tried to relax the muscles on his shoulders. The

more he thought about it, the more likely he decided it was that Angelina was going to marry that man. She always was skittish about serious relationships. All of her worry about having the man investigated was probably a stalling tactic, just something to allow her some breathing room. It was hard for her to trust men. Her father might not have spent much time with her when she was growing up, but he was unerring in his understanding of her.

Tyler unclenched his teeth and smiled at her. He'd call her bluff on this one and contact Clyde.

"I forgot how dry it can be this time of year," Tyler said, feeling the slight movement of air on his face. "It's nice though."

He glanced over at Angelina and she was looking straight ahead.

Clumps of scrub grass covered the ground on both sides of his pickup and the prairie spread out into the distance with a few weeds and some tiny wildflowers showing up here and there. He'd guess they were bluebells. Back down the road a piece, he had seen a desert cottontail rabbit, its brown body crouched low beside a fence post. The blue sky faded to white in the heat of the day.

"There's not too much breeze coming in for you, is there?" he asked her, suddenly realizing he hadn't found out if she minded if he kept his window open a little. He might not be in her social class, but he had always tried to have common courtesy. And women worried about their hair no matter how much money they had. "I know it can be dusty."

"I drive a convertible," she replied, turning to him with a quiet smile. Her hair had fallen into place after her ride to town and he hadn't even seen her pull out a comb.

"Oh." He looked down to see if she had a purse with her that might hold a brush of some kind. That's when he saw she was tapping one foot on the floorboard. It wasn't loud enough to be heard above the engine, but he knew her well enough to know that any kind of foot tapping was a sure sign she was nervous.

"I see someone worked on the road out here," he said as he looked up again. He didn't know what could be wrong. Maybe she was worried he might misinterpret the funeral she was planning for him. He should assure her that he understood she had done it because she remembered him from the past.

Before Tyler could say anything, his eyes were drawn down again. He'd always worn cowboy boots, but he marveled at the sparkly footwear Angelina seemed to find. She had tiny leather straps running over her feet and the largest rhinestones he'd ever seen were cinching the pieces together. At least, he hoped they were rhinestones. With her money, he wasn't sure that they weren't some kind of rare jewel.

He reigned in his thoughts and tried to focus. "My father kept calling the county officials about the road before—"

Angelina's tapping stopped. Tyler winced. He should

have known better than to bring up his father. Not everyone was comfortable being reminded of a man who had been murdered.

"Not everyone knows that the gravel needs to be just right for these roads," Tyler pressed on, turning his eyes completely away from her feet and trying to salvage the conversation.

He could feel Angelina looking at him even though he kept staring ahead.

"For the road to be bladed," he continued, set in his course, "it needs at least four inches of rock and clay mixture. If the rocks are too small they get pushed to the side and nothing is left but dried dirt. If they're too big, they can fly up and hit a car that's following someone. Not that two cars ever meet up on this road anyway. Our ranch is—I mean, was—the only place out this way. Well, except for the Mitchell place and they didn't drive the roads much, either. It was just Amy—she was my brother's girlfriend. Sort of, anyway. And then there was her grandfather and her Aunt Tilly."

"I've met Amy and Aunt Tilly."

Now that he was talking, Tyler realized it was very unusual that a county as poor as this one would have spent money to regrade a gravel road leading to a couple of old ranches, one of them deserted and the other one almost as bad since they hadn't been farming it much even when he left. There was a barbed-wire fence on both sides of the road and somebody must use that land for grazing, but there still wouldn't be enough traffic to justify the price of new gravel.

Then it hit him.

"You didn't pay to have the road done, did you?" He turned to Angelina. "I know you've invited lots of people out to the ranch, but it's not worth having the road repaired just so they have a smooth ride in. They're probably all driving pickups anyway."

She had always thrown herself into anything she did, so Tyler couldn't fault her for that. But he didn't want his funeral to be one of her charity projects. Just because she had money to burn didn't mean she should waste any on him. Better she should pick up another stray dog like Prince.

"I didn't do anything to the road," she assured him stiffly.

"Good."

Then Tyler heard her take a deep breath. "About the road—"

His stomach muscles rolled again.

"I think your brother did," she added softly. "Fixed the road, that is."

That made him brake to a stop, right there in the middle of the road. A couple of sparrows flew up from the tall grass beside the road and a cloud of dust floated up from his wheels.

"My brother? Which one?" he asked, joy racing through him as he turned to her. He'd been meaning to call both of his brothers on the telephone. He hadn't spoken to them for years. They hadn't been close as boys, but he figured that was because they were each trying to survive their father's wrath in their own way. "Was it Jake? He left a few phone messages on a number I had given him, but I was overseas and didn't get them until a week ago. Of course, it could have been Wade, too, I suppose. He wouldn't have my number, but he'd call if he could. Wade's my oldest brother, but Jake's right behind him."

He stopped before he made a blabbering fool of himself.

"I'm sure they'll both be happy to hear from you." She turned to look at him then. Her blue eyes were kind and somewhat earnest. "In fact, they're at the ranch now."

"Here?" Now that was good news, Tyler thought.

She nodded and hesitated again. "Along with your mother."

Tyler was glad he'd already stopped the pickup. He would have run into the ditch otherwise.

"They let my mother come? Here?" he said, relief flooding him. Then he realized. "Oh, of course—because of the memorial service."

He'd heard of prisoners being given a compassionate leave to attend such events. His mother had to be near the end of her sentence anyway. The judge had gone light on her after news of all of his father's abuse had come out in the trial. Tyler decided it wasn't so bad to have this whole mix-up if it gave his mother a few days of freedom.

"I hope the memorial service doesn't give her a problem with the authorities. Now that I'm not dead or anything. Surely they'll know it wasn't intentional."

He turned to Angelina for confirmation. Her eyes were so somber he wondered if his mother was in more trouble than he knew. Then Angelina reached over and put her hand on his arm. He didn't flinch even though it was his bad arm and he wondered if he wasn't feeling the burn all over again.

"They released your mother last Christmas," Angelina said quietly. "She's free for good. And she has other news, but I'll let her tell you that."

Tyler blinked suddenly. He reached over with his good arm to pat Angelina's hand. He started the pickup again. And then he remembered.

"They really think I'm dead? My whole family?"

Angelina looked miserable, but she nodded.

"I'm so very sorry," she stammered. "When Mrs. Stevenson—you remember her? My father's secretary. Well when she finally told me about the death notice, I had to come here and tell someone you'd died. I didn't know who I'd find, whether you had any family left here or not. But it didn't seem right for you to die and no one even know about it."

She spread her arms at that. "You grew up in this part of the country. It's your home.

"Oh." She stopped and brought her arms back to her sides. "I put an obituary in the Billings paper, too."

He swallowed at that. But what was done was done. And he was going to see his family.

Giving him a memorial service wasn't the worst thing a person had ever done to him. And she meant well. One thing he'd say for Angelina is that she had a heart of gold.

She still sat across from him with her head down so he reached over with his right hand and ruffled her hair like he used to. "It's all right, Angel."

"You remember?" She looked up at him in surprise.

"Of course, I remember." Was there something he was missing? "It wasn't much of a code name. Not like they have with the Secret Service. But it worked when we needed it to—"

Tyler thought she would be pleased that he had remembered something like that. But she looked aghast so he added, "I never told your father we had a secret code name or anything. It wasn't like 'dear' or 'sweetheart' or anything anyway. It was strictly business. Just between us."

"You never thought of me as your angel?" she asked, her face pinched.

"Well, no," he stammered. "I knew I was your bodyguard and nothing more. I'd never presume to—that is, I'd never take advantage of our relationship. Not that we had a relationship. It was a business arrangement more than anything even though it did get me through that last year of high school."

Tyler kept digging himself a deeper hole until finally he wondered if he hadn't dug too far. "Not that I didn't consider you a friend." That didn't seem enough, either, so he added, "A very kind friend."

Angelina was just staring at him.

"I get it," she finally said. "You would have taken a bullet for me, but only because it was your job."

Tyler flinched. "I wouldn't say only, but I *was* getting paid to protect you."

She nodded and sighed. "I know. It's just when you threw that knife at the van tire that day—well, it was magnificent, and I couldn't even see all of it. You were like a superhero. All my friends said so. The ones who were standing there and watching it all. My friend, Kelly, still talks about it."

She looked at him fully now and there was a softness in her eyes that made him want to protect her all the more. She didn't need to know he would have taken a bullet for her even if no one had paid him a dime.

"If I'd been paying more attention, they never would have snatched you off the street like that," he said instead. "I would have had time to call in the backup guards and it would have been handled without all the excitement."

They were both silent for a moment, remembering those days.

"It was still very brave." She sighed. "How'd you learn to throw a knife like that anyway?"

"Rattlesnakes," he answered, thankful to move the conversation along. "You have to be quick and deadly if all you have is a knife and you're facing a rattler. Growing up here, I always kept a small knife in my boot."

"You still have the knife?" she asked.

He nodded and puffed his chest up just to amuse

her. "Still have the boots, too. You see any rattlesnakes around, you let me know."

Finally, he got a smile out of her.

Neither of them said anything as he drove the rest of the way to the dirt road that turned off the main gravel road and led up to his family's old ranch.

He stopped just after the turn. Someone had been busy. The field to the right had been plowed and planted this year. Tall stalks of wheat went back deep in the acreage. He wondered how they were controlling the grasshoppers. On the left side of the driveway, the ground was freshly turned. He'd guess someone was going to plant something else there. And in the distance, behind the barn, he saw a herd of cattle, some of them with calves. The place had never looked so good.

His brothers weren't just home, they were working the land. And then he saw a house. No, two houses in the far field. He wondered if his brothers had sold some of the ranch.

"They'll be happy to see you," Angelina whispered as she sat there with him.

He glanced down before she could see the dampness in his eyes. Even if some of the land was gone, he was glad to see his family on this ranch again.

Just then he heard a thump from behind and he turned around to see the dog leap to the ground.

"Prince!" Angelina rolled down her window and called out, but it was too late.

The mutt was off and running, with so much joy

evident in his whole body that Tyler had to smile. "He looks like he's home."

"But he can't live here," Angelina protested. "I rescued him."

"He won't be happy going back to Boston," Tyler said. "Not if he's used to running around in the country here."

"I'm still here for another month."

"Well, you're going to break his heart when you leave. That's all I have to say."

Tyler didn't dare think about his own heart.

Angelina sat in the pickup. "Do you think I'm being selfish? Wanting to keep Prince with me?"

"You'll need to ask Prince. Maybe he'd like to see the ocean."

"Everybody should have a dog."

By then, Prince had run all the way up to the house and another dog came out from behind the barn, barking. Prince didn't seem to mind the other dog and he started chasing what looked like a Rhode Island Red hen that was now running toward the barn. Angelina smiled as the chicken slipped inside the slightly open door at the side of the building.

Prince nosed at the door, but couldn't get it to move so he turned his attention to the three pickups parked next to the house.

"I don't want to startle everyone," Tyler said then, looking over at her. "Maybe you should go inside first and tell them to all sit down, at least."

"That's what I told them to do when I told them you were dead." Angelina wished she could take that conversation back. "I don't want to make them think something else is wrong."

Tyler stopped his pickup next to the other vehicles. "I'm surprised no one's come outside yet. Maybe they're not here."

Angelina shook her head. "They are probably just upstairs in your room getting your boyhood treasures for display. We were going to show them tonight at your service."

"My marbles." Tyler looked at her. "That's all I ever had. Who would want to see my marbles?"

"Well, people do that at funerals. We wanted to give everyone the sense of who you were growing up here. At first I thought of a slide show, but your brothers didn't have pictures of your childhood."

"Of course not. Didn't you hear about the Stone boys? We were fortunate to survive childhood. We didn't have any picture-worthy moments."

"Well, yes, I know, but we wanted to celebrate your life tonight. We had to have some good times to talk about. There must be something."

"Mrs. Hargrove gave me a plate of chocolate chip cookies once when I snuck into her Sunday school class. I think she meant them for the whole class, but she just scooped them all into a bag and gave them to me. I was supposed to be hunting rattlers down in the coulee, but I rode our horse into town and went into the church basement just before she started talking. I'll never forget the look on her face. She was really surprised."

"Well, see, that's a good memory."

"Later, she offered Jake a whole pie if he would go. I almost figured I'd come in second best on that one."

"Life isn't about measuring how much you have against how much someone else might be given." She might sound a little pompous, but she had to say it. She was turning her life around and that was an important part of it.

Tyler grunted. "Easy for you to say when you can have all the pie in the world just waiting for you."

"As a matter of fact, it's not easy for me to say," Angelina protested. "And maybe I don't always have all the pie."

She'd known for a long time that money didn't buy happiness. But she was just coming to understand that the loneliness she felt when she looked at loving families was the same kind of ache that other girls had in high school when they looked in her closet and thought she had every pair of designer jeans in the universe. It wasn't just the missing of the other thing—whether it was clothes or money or loving parents—it was when the lack of that one thing tricked a person into feeling like they were not important to God. That's when people were in trouble.

Just then Prince found another chicken and started to bark again.

"Maybe you should be going," Tyler said to her as he looked toward the dog. "I don't think my brothers will put up with much more barking before one of them comes to see what's going on. The cattle could have gotten out."

Angelina nodded. "Follow close behind me. It'll only take me a minute to tell them."

She opened the door and stepped down to the ground. Without the shade of the cab, the sun beat strong on her. She started walking to the house and, just before she arrived at the side porch, she turned to look back at Tyler. She remembered how difficult it had been to come to the Stone ranch when she first arrived in Dry Creek. If only she had waited to tell everyone that Tyler had been declared dead, she wouldn't have put his family through the grief of it all.

She squared her shoulders as she knocked at the door.

Lord, help me do this right this time, she prayed as she stood there waiting for someone to answer.

Mrs. Hargrove had assured her she could pray to God about any of the struggles in her day. Prayer was new to Angelina, but she had started asking God to guide her even when she didn't know how to pray.

Angelina heard footsteps and took a second to motion for Tyler to come. She was sure his family would want to see him the very minute that she announced he was alive.

It would be like Lazarus bursting forth from his tomb, she assured herself, recalling the story she'd just read with Mrs. Hargrove in the Gospel of John. Then she heard someone start to turn the knob on the door.

*They were all happy to see Lazarus, weren't they, Lord?
Help me to do this the right way.*

She was certainly happy Tyler was alive.

Chapter Three

Tyler wondered what people would have remembered about him if he had died in that bomb blast. He had no land to claim him. No wife to mourn him. He didn't even have a dog like Prince to howl at the moon in his absence.

He frowned, realizing he could have done more to keep in touch with his brothers and his mother. Some people thought hard times brought people together, but his father's rages had destroyed his family. Birthday cards and Christmas greetings had seemed too impersonal after all they had gone through together. Tyler had been in a group foster home for juveniles with his brother, Jake, for several years so he'd seen him for that time. Then, once he was out of there, Tyler had sent money to his mother from time to time, but his messages had been short and full of forced cheer. He'd gotten his job with Brighton Security with a referral from the foster home, but he didn't want to talk to his mother about that. He never knew what to say to someone who was in prison.

When Tyler saw someone open the door for Angelina, he decided it was time to get moving. It wouldn't take her long to explain that the news of his death had been premature. He took a moment to adjust his shirt collar so it would hide more of his burn scar. He didn't want his mother to worry.

Prince came over to run around him as Tyler started walking up to the house. He liked to listen to the crunch of his boots on the hard dirt. He'd gotten used to not hearing footsteps in the sand of Afghanistan, but it made him feel disoriented. He was a Montana man and glad to hear some sound again, especially on his family's ranch.

Tyler kept looking around and noticed someone had been busy with the buildings. Growing up, he always remembered this old house as being in need of paint. It had been built by his father's great-grandparents. Every winter, more white paint would flake off and more of the gray in the boards underneath would shine through. His mother had suggested once that they paint the house, but his father said he didn't have time for all that scraping. He wanted to wait until the winter weather took all of the paint away and then, he said, he'd be happy to slap some new paint on.

Tyler wondered if the flaking had happened like his father had predicted. If it had, someone had put on a light peach color in its stead. It looked good with the white trim on the windows and porch. Looking down, he saw a border of rocks framing a raised flower bed that grew a few purple plants. And, if he wasn't mistaken, his mother's old Christmas rose was still alive at the far corner of the house.

His mother loved flowers and her lilac bushes were green and healthy. Most of the blooms were usually gone by this time in the summer, and he couldn't find their scent so there had been no recent flowers. He was happy that his mother had been released in time to enjoy her lilacs this spring.

Tyler stepped onto the porch, walked through the screened-in area and faced the back door of the house. Someone had taken a paintbrush to this door, too, and it was white. Whoever it was had put a lot of effort into making it look nice and that made him feel good. It honored the whole place.

Tyler realized he was just standing in front of the door, stalling. He didn't know if he should knock or just wait a minute and slip into the kitchen. He could hear people talking, but he couldn't make out what they were saying. He didn't want to startle anyone by appearing before Angelina had time to tell them what had happened.

Finally, he decided to open the door just a little so he could hear where she was in her explanation.

"It's too nice to keep out in the barn," a man's voice said.

Tyler wasn't sure which of his brothers was talking, but it sounded like a few people might be gathered in the kitchen.

"Well, of course, we can't keep it there," another

man's voice responded. "I'm just saying we don't want to put it in the cemetery on top of Dad's grave. People will think its Tyler resting underneath it."

"You're right. We can't do that to our baby brother," the other voice agreed.

"Before you do anything," Angelina said, and Tyler could hear the stress in her voice, "I have an announcement—"

"Could you pass me that pitcher of water first?" his mother asked. She sounded hoarse. "I'm a little dry."

Tyler smiled. He recognized her voice; it had always had a lilting quality to it.

"Of course," Angelina said. "Let me pour it for you."

"I'm going to miss him, you know," one of his brothers said, sounding mournful.

"I know what you mean," the other brother answered. "We haven't seen him for a while, but the world was a better place with him in it."

Now that's what a man likes to hear when he's dead, Tyler thought to himself in satisfaction. He wouldn't want to cause his family any prolonged grief, but it was nice to know he would be missed. He wasn't so sure about the baby brother comment, but the overall tone was nice.

"Actually, there's no need to miss him," Angelina said, her voice brighter now.

"Well—" One of his brothers started to protest.

"He's here," Angelina finished quickly.

There was a pause.

"You mean because of the gravestone?" the other

brother asked. "It's nice and everything, but I've never believed a man's spirit comes back and hangs around any place."

Someone pushed their chair back and Tyler could hear the squeak it made on the linoleum.

"Your great-grandfather would have believed," his mother said. "But then he was pure Cherokee. And the Bible doesn't give us any reason to think the dead stay on the earth as spirits. As nice as the sentiment is, though."

"I don't mean his spirit." Angelina's voice grew more desperate as she went on. "Tyler is here. Alive. With us."

Now, there was absolute silence. It never was easy to tell the Stone family anything, Tyler thought with a grin. Once they had their minds made up to grieve, they would stay the course no matter what anyone said.

"It does seem that way, doesn't it?" his mother finally said, her voice polite.

"I almost thought I heard his footsteps a minute ago," one of his brothers added cautiously. "He used to love those boots of his. I wish we had them. We could bury them under that gravestone and it would be almost like he was here."

Well, Tyler told himself, there was never a better moment to enter a conversation. He opened the door and stepped inside the kitchen. Angelina had done as she said and had everyone sitting around the table that stood in the middle of the kitchen. Unfortunately, she was the one facing him and the others were looking down, probably not wanting to talk anymore about how he was or wasn't there.

"Nobody's going to bury my boots," Tyler said.

His mother gasped so hard it sounded like a squeal. Jake spilled the glass of water he had in his hand. Wade half stood from his chair, looking startled and fierce.

Tyler glanced around quickly. The kitchen had been his favorite room in the house because that's where his mother usually was. It had been painted light green since he'd been here last and it smelled like cinnamon. The appliances were all white and looked new. Someone had painted a red bird on the wall by the refrigerator.

"I paid good money for my boots," Tyler finally said, standing there grinning. "They're not going into the ground."

"Well, praise the Lord!" his mother whispered. Tears were starting down her cheeks.

Tyler nodded and took a step closer to her. She stood then and turned to embrace him.

"It's okay," he said as he felt her tremble in his arms. She seemed more fragile than he remembered. He hoped she couldn't feel the weakness in his left side. She had enough to worry about without adding him to her list.

As soon as he stepped back to give his mother room to breathe, Jake was there, hugging him. Then Wade stood beside them, slapping them both on their shoulders. Fortunately, he'd chosen Tyler's right shoulder so he didn't hit the burn area.

"Easy," Angelina said as she stood up then. She took a step closer to them. "His shoulder is hurt."

Jake and Wade both stepped back.

"Oh, I'm sorry," Wade said, looking stricken. "I never thought."

His brothers looked at him as if he was going to fade away.

"I'm okay," he hastened to say. "Just a little—accident."

Everyone just kept looking at him.

"I heard it was a bomb," Jake finally said. Then he turned to Angelina. "In fact, she told me it was a bomb."

Tyler could see where this was going. "Angelina only passed on what the military sent to her father's firm."

His mother was starting to frown as he talked.

"But that's what I never understood," she said. "Isn't the military supposed to notify your next of kin?"

"I didn't want to bother you," Tyler explained. "So I listed Brighton Security as my next of kin."

"Not bother me—" his mother said, her voice rising. "I'm your mother. I'm supposed to be bothered if you're dead."

"And just who is this Brighton Security?" Wade demanded. "If you didn't want to put Mom down as your next of kin, you should have listed me."

"I didn't have anyone's address," Tyler said in his defense. Maybe he'd taken his independence too far, but he never thought the military would need to contact someone anyway. "And Brighton Security is where I work."

"But that's—" His mother still sounded confused. "Isn't that Angie's last name?"

"Angie?" Tyler didn't understand. "You mean Angelina?"

Even in high school, Angelina had never allowed anyone to shorten her name. Not that many tried. He turned to look at her now.

"I didn't want to be different," she said. "Everybody here is Amy or Susie or Mary or something short. Even your mom is Gracie Stone."

All he could do was shake his head. Here Angelina was, a bona fide rich society woman, and she wanted to sound like she'd grown up in Dry Creek. Kids here spent their summers dreaming about going to the big city. He could suddenly sympathize with her father. Mr. Brighton had worked for decades to give his daughter every advantage possible, and all she wanted was to blend into a small Western town like Dry Creek.

"I think I need to sit down," Tyler said as he walked over to the chair Wade had been sitting in. He looked at his brother. "I hope you don't mind."

"Anything for you," Wade said.

Tyler closed his eyes, feeling tired. The doctors had warned him he'd have some bad days for a while, even before he began his physical therapy. He doubted they'd counted on this kind of a day, though.

"I should make you some tea," his mother said.

Tyler nodded, not bothering to open his eyes.

He could hear his mother's footsteps as she walked over to the stove. So Tyler opened his eyes again. That's when he looked straight across the table and through the doorway into the living room.

"What in the world is that?" he asked in astonishment.

A large pink slab of what looked like marble stood in the middle of the living room. If it had been a few feet shorter, he might have thought it was a coffee table. It had to be four feet high, though, and it had something on one corner.

Everyone was silent.

"It's your gravestone," Angelina finally said.

"For *me*?" Tyler asked, peering at the thing in suspicion. "But it's pink. Real *pink*."

"Pink is a perfectly natural color for a gravestone," she said, her lips pursing together.

"It's okay if you're a girl, I guess," Tyler said, trying to be nice.

"Gravestones are not gender specific," Angelina said. "You can be a man and have a pink gravestone. Well, okay, maybe the cowboys around here will tease you a little," she conceded. "The description said light mauve so I thought—"

"No, this is definitely pink," Tyler said as he shook his head.

"Well, it wouldn't have been a problem if—" she stopped then.

"—if I'd been really dead," he finished for her. "No one would say anything if I'd been dead."

Even the Elkton ranch hands would have sat around with respectful looks on their face and not dared mention the color of the gravestone if he'd been genuinely deceased. There wasn't much that was off-limits in their teasing, but being dead was one of them.

Suddenly, the whole thing made him start to smile. Before he knew it, he had wrapped his arms around Angelina in a bear hug and she was laughing, too.

"I don't know what's so funny," Jake finally said. "They're going to tease you, you know."

Tyler nodded. "I know. I'm alive and it's pink—and it's mine."

Angelina relaxed. Tyler still had his arms around her and she was happy. She laid her hand on his chest just for the pleasure of it. Then he put his hand on her head and patted her.

She sighed. It wasn't that long ago that she'd seen him tap Prince on the head in just the same way. She figured that was her cue to step back and remember they weren't still in high school.

It was suddenly very quiet in the house. Angelina looked around and saw that Tyler's family was staring at them. Well, mostly staring at her.

"I am so sorry," she said.

"You're mighty friendly with a guy you were so eager to bury," Jake said.

"She never did plan to bury me," Tyler said in her defense. "Just memorialize me. And you were the one who wanted to plant my boots six feet under. Good leather they are, too."

"The important thing," Angelina said, "is that unless anyone knows how we can get the word to everyone, I'm guessing there will be a party here tonight."

"Oh, that reminds me," Tyler's mother said. "Mrs.

Hargrove called and she won't be able to come by until tonight. It'd be a pity to cancel anything now, though."

With that, Gracie stepped away from the stove. She had a steaming pot of tea in her hands and she was balancing it carefully as she walked toward the table. The air smelled of orange and spices.

Jake nodded as he walked over to the cupboard. "Besides, we'll want to ask for some help to move the gravestone. It's so fancy it will really stand out in the Dry Creek cemetery. They'll think someone famous died."

Jake pulled a handful of cups down from the top shelf of the cupboard and started carrying them back to the table.

Tyler frowned as he stood up. "Is that where you were going to put me? I thought maybe you could just set me out by Mom's lilac bushes. I'd like it there."

"We can't do that," his mother protested. "The chickens would be all over that stone roosting and making a mess of it. They're worse than pigeons."

"Speaking of birds, is that what this is?" Tyler started walking toward the living room.

Angelina's breath caught as she saw where he was headed. She hurried over to the doorway that separated the two rooms. The curtains were drawn in there and she had hoped the shadows would hide the full sight of the gravestone.

"What's this?" Tyler asked again as he entered the living room.

"Don't—" Angelina followed him into the room although she had no idea how to stop the scene that was unfolding.

"Why, it's an angel!" Tyler pointed at the corner of the gravestone.

"It was just a little extra something," Angelina said.

Wade snorted. He was standing in the doorway now. "That little custom piece cost two thousand extra dollars. It said so right on the receipt."

"Well, I—" Angelina began, and then gave up. She had no excuse.

Lord, she prayed, *I'll never do something like this again—ever. Just help me now.*

Tyler was studying the angel as if he was trying to decipher something. Finally, he walked over to the doorway between the living room and the kitchen.

"Excuse us," Tyler said, and then he reached over and shut the door between the two rooms.

"But Wade—" Angelina protested.

"He can wait on the other side," Tyler said firmly. "This is just between me and you."

And then he walked closer to her.

Angelina stood still. The curtains in the living room were heavy and, when they were closed like this, they filtered the afternoon light until it gave everything a golden glow. The gravestone stood like a giant misfit in the modest room with its one beige sofa and three matching chairs.

Finally, Tyler was standing right in front of her. His eyes were dark and she couldn't read them. Locks of black hair fell down his forehead, but he didn't brush them away. The stubble on his face made him look rugged.

"I plan to have carpet people come in when we've moved the stone," Angelina said nervously and looked down at the floor like she was inspecting the brown carpet. "It's probably going to leave a mark there even when we take the gravestone out."

"That angel is you, isn't it?" he asked gently. "It looks like you. The cheekbones. And the smile. You sent them a picture, didn't you?"

She could do nothing but nod in confession. "I know it sounds odd, but—"

"I think it's sweet." Tyler reached out to touch her cheek.

She felt the softness of his thumb as he lifted her face until she was looking at him. His eyes had warmed and the way he looked at her made her tremble slightly.

"I just didn't want you to be alone in the grave," she whispered, not taking her eyes off his. "I know we didn't actually have your body, but—"

"That's the nicest thing anyone has ever done for me," Tyler interrupted her stuttering, and then he bent down and kissed her.

She had dreamed in high school about getting a kiss like this, but she wasn't prepared for the shot of pure joy that went through her. His lips were soft, but commanding at the same time. Tyler liked the angel. He liked her.

"I'd do anything for you," she said.

He smiled even more. "You're just paying me back for that bullet I promised to take for you."

"I do owe you," she murmured. "But—"

"That's it!" Tyler said suddenly and his voice changed. He stepped back and put one hand up to his head like he should have thought of this before. "I knew there was something suspicious about this assignment."

"You believe my father is being blackmailed?"

"No, but I believe I'm being taken for a ride."

"Huh?" Angelina said, confused.

"You were right to be suspicious. Your father knew you wouldn't be able to refuse me anything so that's why he hired me back."

Angelina frowned. "You're the best security man in the business. I don't think that's what's wrong with my father."

Tyler shook his head. "Maybe I was pretty good in the past. But look at me now—"

He spread his hands and she could see how awkward the left one was.

"Yes, but—"

He didn't wait for her to finish. "I'm so injured that I wouldn't be much use in a kidnapping or even a fist-fight on the playground. My right hand is my gun hand so it's okay, but my left isn't."

"You'll get better," Angelina murmured when he paused. "There's physical therapy. And you always said good security started in a person's brain anyway."

"I couldn't figure out why he gave me my old field job back," Tyler said, and then he looked at her. "He could have offered me a desk job, but he was using me."

"Well, he did hire you."

Tyler shook his head. "No, there's a difference. He was using me to get to you. He knew you felt you owned me for the past."

"I also care about you." She put her heart in the words without stopping to decide whether she should.

"In high school you cared about everybody."

She bit back her breath. "I'm different now. Changed."

"Well, you don't owe me," Tyler said fiercely as he turned and put a hand on each of her shoulders. He looked her squarely in the eyes. "I did what I did in high school because I was paid to do it. I got lucky with a knife throw and I managed to backtrack and get that stalker arrested. I didn't do anything any other body-guard wouldn't have done."

Angelina looked back at him and couldn't help herself.

"You danced with me," she whispered. "So I wasn't left standing out on the floor all alone. No other body-guard would have done that."

With those words, she turned away. She didn't want him to see her blinking back her tears, but the grave-stone blocked her from going farther back into the house. So she lifted her head and walked right past Tyler. When she got to the door of the kitchen, she opened it and walked through.

Tyler's family was gathered at the table. They had clearly been listening. She could tell by their flushed faces.

"I need to go back to the Elkton ranch and fix supper for the men," she said with as much dignity as she could muster. "But I'm afraid my car is in Dry Creek."

Jake stood up and reached into his pocket, pulling out a set of keys. "Here. Take my pickup. It's the blue one."

She nodded, accepting the keys. "I'll be back in time to help get the food ready for tonight."

"Take your time," Tyler's mother said. "Now that it's just a party, people will wander around for a bit first and catch up on the gossip."

Angelina nodded again.

"We'll still want to do the program, though," his mother added. "I know some people have been working all week on what to say. They deserve a chance to put their words out there."

"We can drape a blanket over the gravestone if you want," Angelina said. "I'll ask some of the ranch hands if they can help move it tomorrow."

Jake nodded. "No sense in working tonight."

She heard a footstep behind her.

"Angelina," Tyler called softly. She turned.

He stood there in the doorway between the living room and the kitchen, half in shadow and half in light. He was her friend; she had no doubt of that. And she owed him, no matter what he might think. She didn't owe him for the bullet, though, and that was why he was standing there. He didn't believe there could be more between them. She doubted he even wanted there to be more.

"I'll see you later, Tyler," she said, trying her best to keep her voice even. He wasn't to blame for her girlhood fantasies. He'd been her hero. That had been her fault. And, after the way she behaved in high school, she didn't blame him for not taking her seriously. "I'd appreciate it if you would still make that call to your friend, Clyde."

Without waiting for him to acknowledge that, she nodded to his mother and brothers. "Seven o'clock still?"

They were silent and she took that as agreement so she walked over and opened the door. The afternoon heat met her as she stepped outside, but she didn't care. It would only dry her tears more quickly. She had come to Dry Creek for closure. It looked like she was going to find it.

Chapter Four

Tyler watched the door close behind Angelina. He knew he had to let her leave, but he felt empty inside when she did. He listened until he heard her footsteps cross the outside porch. When she didn't turn back, he looked up and saw his family staring at him. Maybe he was mistaken, but it didn't seem like they were that happy that he had come back right now.

"What did you do to that poor woman?" Wade demanded.

Jake just stood there with his arms crossed. When either of his brothers got angry, they showed their Cherokee heritage by the way they stood, like they were ready to do battle. Tyler supposed he did the same. It was the Stone family way.

His mother was frowning, but she at least looked like she was willing to listen.

"Now, boys," she said in the soothing way she had, "I'm sure Tyler has an explanation."

Then she looked at him expectantly and he felt worse

than ever. His reaction hadn't had much to do with any well thought out reason. The nearest he could figure was that he was nervous about Angelina feeling anything for him. She was like the driven snow, pure and distant. He was like the dirt that got stirred up outside during the spring rains. Her feelings wouldn't last; they never did. And he wasn't a good husband for any woman given his background and now his injury.

"She's practically engaged to some lawyer back in Boston," he finally said, trying to keep the misery out of his voice. "She has the dress and everything."

"Practically engaged?" Wade finally said. "In rodeo, we don't call that a win."

"In poker, we don't even call it a draw," Jake added.

His mother had stopped frowning, but now she was watching him with concern in her eyes. "Have you told her how you feel?"

He started to protest that he didn't feel anything, but he figured his brothers wouldn't accept that.

"We live in different worlds. She drives an Italian sports car that cost a hundred thousand dollars," he tried to explain. "I have the same pickup truck I bought for five hundred dollars the year before I went into the military. The shocks are bad and I have to put a blanket over the seat covers to keep the springs from catching on anyone's clothes. I'm surprised she agreed to ride out here in the thing."

"So it's about a car?" Wade asked, sounding bewildered now. "You can use my pickup."

Tyler gave up and shook his head. "I just don't want her to feel like she *owes* me anything."

"Okay," Jake said slowly. "Did you lend her money or something?"

"No, I saved her life. I was her bodyguard when she was in high school."

"And now?" Jake asked.

Tyler realized there was only one thing he could do to change things. "I need to use the telephone."

"Not a problem," his mother said, smiling. "It's in the living room next to the sofa."

Tyler turned and started to walk. "It's long distance, but I'll pay you back for the charges."

"Talk as long as you want," his mother said.

The living room had grown darker since he left it. The sun was slipping down in the sky and it was just a few hours from dusk. The curtains were closed, but he had no trouble spotting the black dial telephone on the table at the end of the sofa. It looked like the same telephone he remembered from his boyhood.

He sat on the edge of the sofa and picked up the phone. The tone was steady. He knew the number by heart even though it wasn't his usual number for checking in. So, he rotated the dial with his finger. It might be after six o'clock in Boston, but the staff put in long hours.

"Good evening, Brighton Security," a woman's cheerful voice answered.

"Mrs. Stevenson?" he asked. "This is Tyler Stone, calling for Mr. Brighton."

"Oh, Tyler," the woman said, her pleasure plain in her voice. "Have you located Angelina yet? How is she doing?"

"She was fine the last I saw her." Tyler figured there was no need to reveal Angelina had been crying. "I'll tell her you said hello."

"Please do that. And tell her that her wedding dress arrived. She has one more fitting to get done and then all of the adjustments will be made. It'll be perfect for her."

"The dress in the photo?"

"Why, yes." She sounded surprised. "I forgot Mr. Brighton said he'd given you the photo. Isn't it a gorgeous dress? Angelina looks beautiful in it, don't you think?"

"It sure is something," Tyler said, hoping that was sufficient. Angelina wasn't as disinterested in Derrick as she claimed if she was having a wedding dress altered. Not that the fact changed what he needed to do.

"I see Mr. Brighton now," Mrs. Stevenson said. "I'll let him know you're on the phone."

Tyler had to wait for a minute until he heard the click that indicated someone else had come on the line.

"When are you bringing my little girl home?" Angelina's father bellowed into the phone.

Tyler looked up from where he sat on the sofa and noticed the marble angel was staring right at him. "Well, sir, the thing is that Angelina has some commitments in Dry Creek—"

"Commitments! I thought you were supposed to stop all of that nonsense. What am I paying you for then?"

Mr. Brighton's voice was hoarse and he sounded out of breath.

"I don't know, sir. You tell me."

"What are you talking about?"

"Did you send me out here because you knew Angelina would agree to anything I asked simply because she has this idea that she owes me something for saving her life?"

"So what if I did? You think I get results by not playing my best card. I don't care how you persuade her, just get her on a plane and bring her home. I'll take it from there."

Tyler heard the sound of a truck driving toward the house. "Did you have anyone run a background check on this Derrick?"

"Of course not. I know Derrick."

"Angelina thinks he might be blackmailing you and that's why you're pressing her to marry him."

"I've never heard such nonsense in my life."

"So you wouldn't object to me asking for an investigation on the man?"

"Just get Angelina back here and we'll all sit down and talk. There'll be a big bonus in it for you, too."

"How big?"

There was a moment of silence. "One hundred thousand dollars."

Tyler's heart sank. That had to be a bribe. "I can't do that. I'm quitting."

"What do you mean?" Mr. Brighton demanded. "You can't quit until I say so. Your assignment isn't done until you fill out the paperwork. And there'll be no bonus for you, either."

"With all due respect, sir, I don't think—"

"If she won't come here, I'm flying there to talk some sense into her. She's my daughter and needs to start acting like it. Book me a couple of rooms at the best hotel in this Dry Creek place. I'll be there on Sunday," Mr. Brighton said.

"I'm afraid there's not—" The line went dead.

Tyler hung up the phone and just sat there. He expected someone would tell his ex-employer that there were no hotels in Dry Creek. Tyler had other things to worry about. Right now, he agreed with Angelina that the bushes were moving. Something had her father scared. It wasn't unusual for him to be demanding. But he never gave anyone a hundred-thousand-dollar bonus.

Tyler picked the phone up again and this time he dialed another number he knew by heart. He'd used Clyde's number as a computer password for a time and he hoped it was still good.

"Clyde?" he said when the phone was answered.

"Tyler? Tyler Stone?" the voice of his friend answered, sure and strong.

As it turned out, Clyde still did a little investigation work on the side. And, since he had contacts all over the financial world, he said he'd be happy to find out if there was any indication Angelina's father was being blackmailed.

"Start with his connection to his attorney, Derrick

Carlson," Tyler told him. "And I need the information fast."

"With our Angelina, that's always the way, isn't it?" Clyde said with a chuckle as he said goodbye.

Tyler turned around and parted the curtain so he could look out the window. A brown delivery truck was almost to the house.

Tyler sat there for a moment, wondering what he was going to do for work now. It galled him that it had taken him so long to see the job offer from Brighton for what it was. He supposed that was why Angelina's father had met him at the airport, too, and driven him to a modest hotel nearby where the man paid for a week's stay, claiming it was a business expense since it was for an employee. The whole thing stung Tyler's pride now that he realized what had been behind it.

"Tyler," his mother called from the kitchen. "You better come out and sign for this."

He walked around the gravestone, stopping only briefly to rub his hand over the angel's head. It reminded him, with a pang, of running his hand over Angelina's much softer hair earlier. He didn't need any intuition to know that was a bad habit to start.

He opened the door to the kitchen and smelled something floral. "Wildflowers."

A half dozen huge flat bowls, filled with the flowers planted in black dirt, covered the whole of the kitchen table. He saw bluebells, morning glories, violets and some Queen Anne's lace. They were a riot of color. Maybe they were his favorite, after all, with their sweet scents. He used to go down in the coulee and pick them for his mother. He wondered if he'd ever told Angelina about the flowers. That's when he first ran into the rattlesnakes.

"I'll need you to sign for these," the uniformed deliveryman said as he held out a clipboard. "I want to get back to Miles City before it's too late."

Tyler took the paperwork and used the pen sitting on top to sign the line on the bottom.

"Whew," he said as he stared at the total bill. It may have been paid by Angelina Brighton, but he hoped there was a hidden discount that he wasn't seeing.

The deliveryman took back the clipboard and read the name. "Thank you, Mister— Hey, isn't that the name of the funeral guy?"

"There was some confusion," Tyler admitted.

"I guess." The man grinned, and then slapped him on the back. "Congratulations on being alive, buddy. What'd you do? Get lost?"

"In a manner of speaking, I suppose."

"Well, you need to sign for this next one, too."

The man folded back the first receipt and showed the second one.

"It's for our classic wreath," he said. "I left it out on the porch."

There was no name listed on the second receipt, but Tyler frowned at the amount. It was more than Angelina's bill. No one around here should be spending that kind of money on him even if he had died.

"Can't you return the thing and credit the money

back?" Tyler asked as the man stepped into the kitchen again, this time holding a huge floral wreath. "It would be unused."

"You're kidding, right?" The deliveryman unfolded a stand and placed the wreath on it. "The boss has a no-refund policy. Of course, that's mainly because of the weddings. They tend to be unpredictable. I don't think anyone's ever tried to cancel a funeral before. Besides, the wreath looks nice. Here you've got your roses, your gladiolus, some lilies, a few hydrangea. It's the deluxe package. Looks great at the gravesite."

A white banner was draped over the wreath with Tyler's name printed in somber black letters.

"Can't you at least tell me who bought it?" Tyler asked. "I'd like to pay them back, especially since I'm not really dead. As you can see."

The man shook his head. "It's anonymous. We probably can't even trace it back. I'm guessing whoever ordered the wreath will be wishing they'd gone for the daisies though. We had a special on daisies. Next time they won't be so fast to order the deluxe package until they verify there's really a body."

"Life's unpredictable, I guess," Tyler agreed. It shouldn't be too hard to find out who had sent the wreath.

"Well, that's that," the man said as he started walking back to the door. "If you ever die for real, remind folks to ask about the specials first. And those flowers should last for a week. The boss put something in the water."

"Good to know," Tyler said as the man left.

Everyone was silent for a moment, just looking at the flowers. There was enough tension in the room to make the hair on the back of Tyler's neck stand up.

"So which of you bought the wreath?" Tyler finally asked.

"I should have—" Wade started.

"I was going to—" Jake added.

Tyler looked at his mother. No one was telling him who had sent the flowers, but he was sure at least one of them knew. His mother just pressed her lips together and shook her head.

"Are you okay?" he asked her. Her color suddenly didn't seem so good, and her eyes were wary. The flowers could wait. "Maybe you should go lie down for a bit. I know there's a lot going on—"

"You could go over to my place and take a nap," Wade offered as he moved closer to their mother. "Amy is there and she'll fix you up."

"Your place?" Tyler asked as he looked up. "You don't just live here with Mom?"

His brothers chuckled at that.

"They are both married now," his mother said, the color coming back to her face. "Jake and Cat have the cutest little girl, Lara. And Wade's Amy is pregnant. They'll all be here tonight."

"Cat from the home where we lived?" Tyler asked Jake, grinning. "You always said you were just friends." Then he turned to Wade. "And you must be with Amy Mitchell, the girl on the place next to us."

"Guilty as charged," Wade said with an answering grin.

"Me, too," Jake said.

"Well, I'll be—" Tyler said, and then paused.

"We each built a house on the ranch," Wade added, and then hesitated. "We picked out a site for you, too. The best view for miles around."

"For me?" Tyler asked. "Why would you give me the best? I wasn't even here."

Wade and Jake exchanged a glance that Tyler didn't understand. Something was definitely going on.

Before he could say anything though, Jake was talking again. "We had the foundation put in and we can finish it up in no time. I have a builder that comes in with a crew and can put up a house in a month. Just give us the word and I'll schedule it."

"I don't know—"

"Don't worry about the cost. We'll work out something later. All you'll need to do is let the builder know what you want. Cabinets. Tile. Colors. That kind of thing. It'll do you good to be settled even if you don't want to live in the house right now."

Tyler was quiet. It was a lot to take in. "You mean we will all work the ranch together?"

Wade nodded. "Limited partnership going four ways. Us three boys and Mom. We're planning to start a line of pure-bred Red Angus this fall. We could use the help if you want to sign up with us."

"I've been working in security. I need to do some physical therapy, but I thought—"

"Ranching isn't exciting enough for you, is that it?"

Wade said, his cheeks flushed and his voice low. "You'd rather get shot at."

"No one's shooting at me."

"They almost blew you up with a bomb," Jake said. "I can still see the burn scars on your neck."

Tyler flushed. "But I don't go out looking for bombs. That wasn't my regular job."

"Even as a kid, you were always out hunting those rattlesnakes," Jake said, shaking his head. "Staying safe was never good enough for you. Mom's been worried sick."

Tyler looked at his mother. "I'm sorry."

"It was as if you always had to prove something—" Wade added. "If I'd been smarter back then, I might have been able to help. You acted like you were invincible."

"I believed in standing on my own two feet and being a man. Nothing wrong with that."

"Now, boys," their mother interrupted, and they all grew quiet. "We'll discuss this later."

The silence was uncomfortable.

"I appreciate the offer anyway," Tyler finally said. He truthfully wasn't sure if he should continue in security. He'd taken the Brighton assignment as proof that others believed he could still do the job but now he knew why Brighton asked him to work. If he stayed and the physical therapy didn't work, he'd have to take a desk job and he didn't want to do that.

"You've proven you're a man," Wade added after a minute. "A hero in fact. And you're going to have to settle down someday. I just want you to know we have a place for you. That's all."

"I appreciate that."

Jake held out his hand. "Welcome home, baby brother."

Tyler shook hands with him.

Wade put his arm around each of them and pulled their heads together. "Just like old times."

"Let's hope not," Tyler said, but he didn't stop grinning.

"Now, all you need is a good woman to marry and—" Jake stopped mid-sentence. He looked at Tyler sheepishly. "Sorry. I always put my foot in it."

"Not a problem," Tyler assured him, but his smile faded.

"Maybe you just need to talk to her," Wade suggested. "I know it's not easy, but—"

Tyler shook his head. "Angelina is tenderhearted, but she and I aren't really—well, it's for the best. Any self-respecting man would find it hard to marry a woman with that much money. I couldn't ask her to live on a salary like I'd have, and I couldn't live on her money."

He let that settle in before he added. "Anyway, I'm not sure marriage is for me. I worked alone, even in Afghanistan. And seeing the way Dad was, maybe it's for the best. Besides, if I stayed here, you all know how hard it is to be a rancher's wife in Dry Creek. The winter snow can make it impossible to get out for weeks at a time. And, even when you do get out, there's no place to go."

"Amy doesn't mind—" Wade finally replied.

"But she grew up around here," Tyler said, and looked at Jake. "How about Cat? Did she stumble into money after she left the home?"

Jake chuckled. "No, pretty much the opposite."

Tyler nodded. "Angelina's favorite food in high school was roasted duck à l'orange followed by crème brûlée. Kids here think they're living high if they get the deluxe burger at the café."

"Don't give up on the one you love," his mother said abruptly, her voice suddenly hoarse. "You'll regret it if you do."

"Oh." Tyler stopped himself from saying anything more. He didn't want to distress his mother.

"Maybe God has brought Angelina here to be with you," his mother continued, looking better than she had. "Maybe you just don't know it yet. He does bless us unexpectedly sometimes."

"What has God got to do with—" Tyler began, and then had a realization. "You've gotten religious."

Tyler had spoken without thinking and he wished he could take the words back.

His mother nodded, beaming now. "He's forgiven me all my failings in life. I want you to know that."

Tyler looked over to his brothers, hoping for help.

"Us, too," Wade said as he lifted his hands in surrender. "We're a brand-new family these days."

Tyler looked around again. "I know our old one wasn't perfect, but isn't this a little extreme?"

"It might take some getting used to," Wade admitted.

Then Tyler saw the light. "That's why you saved the best for me! You're feeling guilty because Dad always favored the two of you and—"

His mother froze in place, her face suddenly pale again. Wade and Jake both looked like they were ready to bolt.

"It's okay," Tyler said softly. "I knew I was the youngest. I figured my time would come."

No one answered and it was so quiet Tyler began to wonder.

"Was there more? Not just that I was the youngest?"

Tyler could hear the ticking of the clock as it hung over the refrigerator.

"Dad didn't—" Wade said softly. "He wasn't the kind of man to forgive anything."

"So what did I do?"

"We'll talk later," his mother interrupted, more forceful than she'd been yet. "We don't want to ruin the—" She stopped, too, suddenly looking short of breath.

"—my memorial service," Tyler finished for her.

Wade grunted but, other than that, it was silent.

"It's just that Angelina has gone to so much work," his mother said softly. "We have to try to have a good time."

Tyler nodded. "Anyone have an antacid tablet?"

Jake reached into his shirt pocket and pulled out a roll.

Tyler accepted the tablets.

"Take two if you want them to work," Wade suggested.

Tyler nodded. He probably should take three if he had to pretend to enjoy his memorial service. He hadn't seen anyone in Dry Creek for years. He didn't expect them to welcome him home.

Angelina shifted gears as she left to go back to Gracie's place. She should have known the Elkton ranch hands would demand their biscuits. The sun was low in the sky and she barely had time to return to the Stone place before dark. She was glad she had Jake's pickup because the quiche and stuffed mushrooms took up more room than she had expected. She glanced at the plastic bins in back that held them. Added to that, she had a big tub of crudités—carrots, celery and green pepper strips along with the sauces for dipping—all sitting on the floorboard of the pickup.

Earlier today, she'd boiled a gallon of lemon syrup and had it ready for making lemonade. That, along with the ranch's big percolator coffeepot, was sitting on the passenger seat. She'd made cheese sticks out of some nice cheddar yesterday and they were tucked away inside the coffeepot.

The only good thing about all the lifting of bags, boxes and jars was that she was moving too fast to feel any disappointment about Tyler. That's how she managed sometimes. She'd push back any feelings of loss by laughing and staying busy. She'd learned to do that as a child. If her father didn't make it home for Christmas dinner, she threw herself into solving a thousand-piece jigsaw puzzle or singing along with the radio.

Tyler thought she didn't care about anything because she changed focus so often. But the truth was she cared too deeply. She did what she had to do to keep the pain from touching her. It had been that way since her mother died.

For now, she told herself bracingly as she pulled into the driveway of the Stone ranch, she would be so busy being a hostess that she wouldn't have time to feel bad that her high school dreams weren't coming true.

A few more pickups were parked outside of the house so Angelina parked behind Tyler's vehicle.

Seeing the pickups all lined up reminded her she should ask Mrs. Hargrove for a ride back to Dry Creek later tonight so she could get her convertible.

She heard the kitchen door open as she stepped out of the pickup.

All three Stone brothers were walking toward her.

"We've come to help," Wade said as he looked in the back of the vehicle. "I'm assuming everything goes in."

"Yes, please," she said as she held out the keys to Jake. "And thank you."

She noticed Tyler's hair was damp as he reached down to pull the tub of vegetables off the floorboard.

"You shaved," she said.

She kind of missed the stubble, and then realized it was because he looked a little dangerous with it. Maybe she had romanticized him earlier. There was something about his boots. Kelly had called them his heartbreaker boots. And he did have those dark good looks. His black hair had always fallen across his forehead like he was a biker. And his eyes kept secrets. Any teenage girl would have felt something for him.

When he glanced up now, though, he looked more tired than mysterious. His eyes were serious, maybe even wary. "Figured I better get cleaned up for the party since I'm the guest of honor."

"The party doesn't need to go late." She reached for the gallon of lemon syrup. "People will understand if you want to make it an early night."

She hugged the jar as she started making her way toward the house.

"We know how to party better than that around here," Tyler protested, sounding a little indignant.

Wade had the door open for her before she stepped up on the porch. And Jake came outside and insisted on carrying the jar for her.

"It's not heavy," she said, but Jake had already lifted it out of her arms.

"We know how to treat a lady," he said with a determined smile.

Angelina just stood there then. They were waiting on her as if she were a fragile little princess. She looked at their backs in disapproval.

"I've been working out at the Elkton ranch," she finally muttered.

They didn't hear her, though, and, by this time, Tyler was coming up the steps with the coffeepot. He'd already put the tub of cut vegetables on the porch and it was sitting there ready to be taken inside.

"What did you tell your brothers about me? I know

I got a little emotional earlier today, but I don't need to be handled," she hissed at Tyler.

Tyler set the coffeepot on the floor of the porch and looked at her. "I beg your pardon."

"You wouldn't treat a woman like that who grew up around here," she said as she marched up to the open door. "You'd let her carry things."

The door hadn't been propped open securely and it started to close. She held it for Tyler, and he walked in behind her.

"Thank you for holding the door," he said pointedly as he carried the coffeepot over to the counter by the sink.

"I—" she started, and then shook her head. It was going to be a long night.

When she got inside, she glanced around. Tyler was still by the sink, but everyone else was looking at her.

"Anyone got an antacid tablet?" she asked.

They all eyed each other, but Jake eventually pulled out the roll from his shirt pocket.

"There's only one left," he said as he handed it to her.

"It'll have to be enough."

"I could get you something to drink with that," Wade offered. "We have everything here they would have in a big city."

"Really?"

He winced. "Well, I'd have to drive to my house to get anything. But I think there's a bottle in the cupboard."

Right then, a pleasant-faced blonde came up and took his arm. "That's cooking sherry, dear."

Angelina recognized Wade's wife, Amy, and she smiled at her.

"Oh," Wade said.

"But the water here is good," Jake said.

The door opened again then. The sun was setting and the porch was in shadows. But Mrs. Hargrove was standing there, a grin on her wrinkled face and her short gray hair pinned neatly in place.

"There he is," the older woman said as she stepped inside and looked over to where Tyler stood. "You made it back to us."

She was wearing a polyester dark blue dress. Angelina knew that was unusual for Mrs. Hargrove since she liked the comfort of gingham cotton housedresses. She even had a string of pearls around her neck.

The older woman stepped over to Tyler and gave him a big hug.

"You don't have your apron," Tyler said, with a shy kind of a smile that warmed Angelina's heart. He clearly cared for this woman.

"Don't tell me you want a lemon drop?" Mrs. Hargrove grinned as she reached up to touch his cheek. "I should have brought you one."

"I think I can get by without it."

The two just looked at each other for a minute. Angelina felt herself blinking back a tear. Now, this was why she had planned a funeral for Tyler. He had roots in this community that went deep, whether he acknowledged them or not. She envied him.

"I heard you have been praying for me," Tyler said to Mrs. Hargrove.

The older woman nodded, her face flushed with pleasure.

"Thanks." Tyler's voice was hoarse and Angelina wondered if he was as struck by the love in this room as she was. "I know I'm not—well—the kind of person people usually pray for, but thanks."

"I've been praying for more than your safety," the older woman said softly. "I've been praying you'll turn your life over to God."

Tyler looked down at that and Angelina's heart sank.

Mrs. Hargrove put her hand on Tyler's shoulder. "Think about it. God keeps the door open."

By this time, everyone else had wandered over to the counter in the kitchen.

"You didn't buy me that wreath, did you?" Tyler finally asked the older woman as he pointed into the living room where the flowers rested on the stand. "I want to reimburse whoever bought it."

Angelina followed Tyler's gaze into the living room. At least she wasn't the only one who had been extravagant for the funeral.

Mrs. Hargrove turned to the man who had just entered the kitchen. "You didn't order flowers, did you, dear?"

"Charley Nelson?" Tyler said, recognizing the man. The older man had clearly dressed in his best clothes, black suspenders crossing his white shirt and a red bow tie around his neck. His gray hair was mussed and he had his reading glasses in his shirt pocket.

"I needed to find a place to park our car that was out of the way," Charley said. "We might need to leave early and we don't want to be blocked in."

"You're leaving together?" Tyler asked. "I thought you lived in different directions."

"You probably don't know we got married." The older woman smiled as the two men shook hands. "Charley, bless his heart, lets people still call me Mrs. Hargrove. I've had the name for so long and the children in town were getting all confused so we just let it go. He says it's the heart, not the name, that matters anyway."

The older woman looked so pleased with everything, Angelina almost felt as though she were intruding in something meant to be private. So she took a step away and studied the other people in the kitchen. That wreath had to have been sent by someone close to Tyler. He'd obviously questioned his brothers and mother and, since they were standing there without acknowledging the flowers, it could only mean there was someone else.

"Tyler must have a girlfriend." Angelina hadn't meant to speak the words aloud, and they were so soft she didn't think anyone else could hear.

She glanced around quickly and nobody was looking back at her so she figured no one had caught what she said.

But then Wade turned his head slightly and she knew he'd heard.

"Which is good," she continued, trying to stop his speculation while not alerting anyone else to her unfortunate slip. "Love is always good."

"And the answer is no about the girlfriend," Wade whispered back. "Not unless you count yourself."

Angelina felt herself relax. The antacid seemed to be working.

She heard the sounds of a dozen boots out on the back porch, and then they were quiet. The cowboys were hanging back a little, letting the group in the kitchen finish getting everything done.

"Well, we're almost ready for the guests," she said, loud enough this time so everyone could hear.

"Let the memorial service begin," Tyler said as he opened his arms wide.

"Very funny." Angelina grinned as he made a martyr's face. The evening might be all right, after all. Tyler didn't have a girlfriend.

She suddenly realized she should have promised the cowboys more biscuits. The men around here teased each other unmercifully, but they took their food seriously. It would have distracted them from that gravestone. And the starry look she probably had in her eyes whenever she thought about Tyler.

Not that she had any business dreaming about Tyler. He didn't take her seriously and he was probably right not to do so. Just because he didn't have a girlfriend didn't mean he wanted to see more of her. Besides, she'd lived her life by running away from closeness. She never wanted to feel the pain of losing someone like she had with her mother. Maybe she was just better at casual relationships.

She watched Tyler go into the other room. It was time to begin.

Chapter Five

Tyler was glad when his mother turned the overhead lights off in the living room. He didn't want people to stare at him; he was self-conscious enough just being the honoree at this upside down memorial party. So he stood in the shadow he had found in the corner closest to the kitchen and discreetly looked around. He figured he should be allowed that much.

A lamp sat on the small mahogany table in the other side of the room, along with a bowl of Angelina's wildflowers. The curtains were closed, but it was dark outside by now so the sun would not have provided more light anyway. The lamp cast a golden glow over the room so that people could see each other even though there were gentle shadows. The wreath hung on a stand behind the table, almost like a sentinel watching over the proceedings. Tyler had exhausted his ideas on who might have given it to him, and that bothered him a little.

Someone had pulled the sofa and chairs away from

the wall so there was space for the ranch hands to stand behind the different pieces of furniture. He didn't know the cowboys well enough to count them as friends. But he liked the way they stood in their white shirts and ties with their arms straight down like they were ready to salute. His eyes moved down to the sofa and he saw Mrs. Hargrove sitting with a couple of other older people he didn't know. A few children were seated cross-legged on the floor.

Tyler didn't know most of the ranch women who came. He probably had gone to school with some of them years ago, but he didn't recognize them. They each wore a dark-colored dress and a few of them wore beads of some kind around their necks. His mother spoke to each one so they were known to her at least. He supposed he'd meet them all later although now they were comfortable sitting in various chairs and he didn't want to disturb them.

Once everyone was settled with a place to sit or stand, it started to grow quiet. The people were arranged facing the middle of the room. Angelina had put a large vanilla candle on top of the gravestone and everyone's eyes seemed drawn to the flame. The candle scent drifted around the room mixing with the floral fragrance and Tyler found it pleasant.

His eyes didn't focus on the candle, though. Instead, he found himself gazing across the room at Angelina. She was sitting in one of the wood chairs directly in front of him with her hands folded in her lap. If he didn't know better, he would think she was really grieving. She had her long hair pulled back and piled high on her head. The black dress she wore had floated as she walked around getting everything ready and, now that she was sitting, it settled to her frame like it belonged there.

Angelina donned no sparkle of jewelry and that surprised him. She used to spend hours picking out necklaces and scarves, lipstick and nail polish. She loved that kind of splash. Maybe she truly was in mourning. He wondered if she had some sorrow he knew nothing about. There had been a time when he had been privy to all her troubles, but now he knew little.

As the minutes passed, Tyler heard the few stray whispers die down. Someone coughed quietly. Not everyone had heard that he was still alive and, when someone addressed him by name, a few of the young boys looked at him nervously, no doubt wondering if some of the old ghost stories they'd heard around campfires were to be believed.

Tyler had the urge to say "boo" and tease them.

But he glanced back at Angelina and the strain on her face made him stand straighter and try to look as dignified as he could. He'd always told himself he'd die for her if necessary. Of course, that was the pledge any bodyguard took. She needed something different from him now and the least he could do was be a good sport about tonight.

Wade was the first one to step to the middle of the room. He wore a dark gray suit jacket, which made him look more like a banker than any Stone brother ever should. But Tyler forgave him because he also wore one of his trophy rodeo belt buckles and the calluses on his hands would never have been found on a man who pushed paper for a living. The gravestone made a convenient pulpit, and Wade gently set a big black book on top of it.

"This is our mother's Bible," Wade said by way of beginning. "She asked me to bring it here tonight to show how faith has changed our family."

Then he held the book up and flipped through the pages.

Tyler saw a kaleidoscope of colors flying by on the different pages of the Holy Book.

"As many of you know, Gracie Stone became a Christian in prison," Wade continued. "And she began to read the Bible with her family in mind. The yellow marks are for verses that speak of the truth that God calls each of us to honor. Secrets had destroyed our family and my mother sought the courage to simply tell the truth— about my father's abuse, her own failings and what she knew of his murder. All of these things weighed on my mother's heart until she saw the red marks that show the redemption God has promised each of us."

Tyler swallowed hard. His mother said she had something to tell him, but she had not done so yet. Maybe she knew he had been outside the barn door all those years ago. Maybe she knew he had run away when he should have stayed and helped her.

Tyler forced himself to listen more. He could not go

back and change the past. All he could do was be stronger in the future.

"My mother prayed for her three sons to come home," Wade continued, his voice husky. "The lilac color in her Bible showed the promises and prayers she claimed as her own." He fanned the pages again to reveal the prominence of the color. "And today her prayers were answered."

The silence in the room took on a reverent feel. Tyler swallowed. He had no idea his mother had prayed for him as she had. It was humbling and stirred something inside of him.

Then his mother stood up and carried something over to the gravestone.

"I was planning to bury this under the gravestone," she said as she held up a brown jacket that Tyler instantly recognized. "I know it doesn't look like much to many of you, but it's my most precious possession. It's an old wool coat that belonged to my youngest son. I felt bad that we couldn't get something better for him, but we had no money for new clothes and, when I saw it in the secondhand box outside of the church one day, I asked if I could have it. I could tell by the smell it had been someone's barn jacket. The buttons were all missing and the cuffs were frayed. But I cleaned and fixed it the best I could. And, I was grateful to have it because without it my son wouldn't have had a warm coat."

Tyler had to close his eyes. He could see what his mother was remembering and could almost feel the bite of the snow on that winter day.

"On the afternoon I was arrested, I was so agitated that I had gone outside without getting so much as one of my husband's old flannel shirts to cover my shoulders. When the sheriff started taking me to his car, I didn't even know I was freezing. But my twelve-year-old Tyler stopped Sheriff Wall. He stood right in front of the lawman, with determination in his eyes, and my son took off his coat and gave it to me."

His mother stopped for a moment.

Then she continued with her voice low. "I kept that coat all through my years in prison. It reminded me of my dear, dear son and how much he cared about me. And how he was out there facing the cold all alone."

Tyler opened his eyes when he heard a sob. He looked around, but didn't see who was crying. He wanted to go comfort them, to remind whoever it was that he was alive and his mother was out of prison. No one had frozen to death. But then he figured whoever it was might be weeping for the hardness of their own lives.

That brown coat had always reminded Tyler of the poverty of his family. They never seemed to have enough money for whatever the need had been. Of course, the same could be said for many of the families around here. He was sure most of them had worn hand-me-downs at some point in their lives. And, although they probably called the poor box at the church something else these days, he doubted the clothes collected stayed inside it for long. Somebody always needed something.

He looked across at Angelina and saw sympathy on her face. She had never known what it was to do without warm clothes, but she did seem to understand how it would feel when it happened to the people here.

At that point, Mrs. Hargrove stood up and announced it was time for them to all pray.

Everyone stood and looked expectantly at her.

"Let's join hands," the older woman said, and she closed her eyes without waiting to see if the neighbors in front of her obeyed her command or not.

Tyler was hoping Mrs. Hargrove meant the words figuratively, but he realized everyone was taking her seriously when one of the younger cowboys from the Elkton ranch offered his hand on one side of him and a teenage boy awkwardly offered his hand on the other.

Tyler wasn't sure he should be part of this chain. God would spot a fake; he was sure of that. Tyler feared he might even be the one who disconnected this whole prayer circle, like a bad Christmas tree light did. But, while he hesitated, the people on either side of him seemed to have no time for his doubts. They each grabbed one of his hands and bent their heads in prayer.

They could just as well be taking hold of a doorknob, Tyler told himself in consolation. Prayer wasn't like electricity, he reassured himself. Or a Christmas tree light. He couldn't short the thing out. At least, he didn't think so. The other lights would still shine around him even if he wasn't able to pray.

He frowned at his own thoughts. Did he want to pray?

He wasn't sure why, but that question made him look across the room to where Angelina stood. Just seeing her calmed him. She stood with her head bowed and a look of peace surrounding her. Then he saw her move her lips and he thought she whispered his name.

"Lord," he murmured with her, not realizing he was echoing her prayer.

"Oh," he gasped involuntarily as a tingle of pure power shot through him. He looked at the men on either side of him, but they were still praying earnestly. He looked down at his feet and they were grounded on linoleum. He must have imagined the surge, he told himself.

Still, Tyler figured he should bow his head and pay more attention to the prayer just in case there was something to all of this and God was watching them.

He no sooner thought it than he knew God had to be listening.

Everyone paid attention to Mrs. Hargrove and she was beseeching the Almighty Father of heaven and earth to bless Tyler Stone. Then she asked Him to bring "her boy" into the fold where he belonged.

"Put him right in Your arms, Father," she continued earnestly. "Let him know what it is to have a loving Father after the miserable earthly father he's known."

Tyler wasn't sure that he liked having the abuse in his family brought up in public, but then he realized she hadn't said a word that every person in the room didn't already know. The stories of how his father used to get drunk and beat up on everyone had been common knowledge after his mother's trial. It was hardly a secret now. He thought of all those doors in Dry Creek again and wondered if they had really opened to the press. Maybe the gossip about his family had been there for anyone to see on both sides of the doors. His bruises alone would have told the story.

Mrs. Hargrove paused in her prayer. Tyler wasn't sure if she was finished because no one let go of the hands. Everyone still had their heads bowed, too.

Then Tyler heard a soft footstep behind him. He was standing in the doorway to the kitchen so he figured no one else would have noticed the sound. Since he knew how it felt to come to a meeting late, he opened his eyes and turned his head to at least give the person a welcoming nod.

But then he stopped. The man standing in the middle of the kitchen was staring at him.

It had been many years, but Tyler recognized him. There was some white in the man's brown hair and a few wrinkles around his eyes, but the solid sturdiness in his face was the same as when Tyler had been a boy.

"Calen? Calen Gray?" he whispered.

Tyler unhooked himself from the prayer circle and walked into the kitchen, stretching out his hand toward the man who stood there with a grin on his face.

"I didn't think you would remember me," Calen said as he gripped Tyler's hand and then reached up to remove his worn gray Stetson.

"You bought me my first fishing lure," Tyler said. "Red and white striped. A boy doesn't forget something like that. I still have it, too. In the glove compartment of my old pickup."

The older man flushed in pleasure. "Well, I was getting tired of watching you try to catch one of those granddaddy trout in the Big Dry Creek with nothing but a grasshopper or two for bait."

Tyler kept looking at the man. He had taught him everything there was to know about creek fishing. And he was always patient with Tyler's many questions. And, like as not, the man would bring an extra sandwich if it was a Sunday afternoon and the fish were biting.

"I didn't know you were still around here," Tyler said.

Calen nodded. "I left for a few years, but I've been back at the Elkton ranch for quite a while now. But it won't be for long. I'm the foreman there now, but I'm saving to buy my own place. I've almost got enough, too. I hope to find something by Christmas."

Tyler liked the pride he saw in his friend's face.

"Make sure it has a creek with good fishing," Tyler said. "I'll come visit."

"I'd like that."

"I suppose you know what's going on here."

Calen nodded. "I needed to see for myself that you were alive. And I'm going to hold you to that visit when I get my new place. I'm hoping to find something close around here so it won't be far."

"Well, I'm glad you came tonight."

They were silent for a moment.

"I heard about the bomb," the older man finally said, a frown deepening on his forehead. "Where'd it happen?"

"I was on the Pakistan-Afghanistan border. The tribal people told the officials I was dead. I think they were protecting me. They carried me off to the nearest local hospital and I laid there in a semi-coma for a few weeks. When I finally did make contact with my Special Ops unit, they had already sent out a missing-in-action notice that somehow got translated to me being dead."

Calen nodded like he knew things like that could happen. "Well, I'm glad you're not."

"Me, too."

"I understand our relief cook arranged all this in your honor," the older man continued. "She's a good woman. Good with the men."

Tyler bristled. He didn't mean to, but he changed to a fighting stance almost without thinking.

Calen chuckled. "I see. What I meant is that she doesn't let their teasing upset her. She's a real good sport."

"She's an heiress," Tyler retorted. "She has no business pretending to be a cook."

Calen nodded. "She wanted the job, though, and the men are happy."

"I suppose they are," Tyler said with a grimace.

Calen raised an eyebrow. "I'm guessing it might take more than a fancy lure to catch her. But there's no one more patient than a Dry Creek fisherman."

"I already told you she's—"

Calen interrupted him with a nod. "I know the drill. I've told myself things like that, too. It won't work. It's not for you. She won't say yes anyway. I've told myself all of those things. But—if you want a piece of advice—don't sell your heart short. Hers, either. Love is a mighty fine thing and worth holding on to. Even if sometimes there's not much else you can do."

Just then there was a loud "amen" from the other room.

Tyler looked behind him and saw everyone start to stand up in the living room. Someone flipped the overhead switch and the room flooded with light.

"Well, it looks like—" Tyler said, turning around.

Calen wasn't standing beside him any longer. The man had already walked over to the door and was reaching for the knob. His hat was back on his head.

"Aren't you staying?" Tyler asked.

Calen shook his head. "I need to get back to the ranch. I just wanted to drop in and see that you were really here."

"Well, thanks."

"Happy fishing," Calen said with a smile, and then he walked out the door just as the first of the cowhands came into the kitchen.

"I hear the food's out here," the man said as he held out his hand to Tyler. "Glad you made it home."

After Tyler shook hands, he realized a line had formed. Everyone wanted to congratulate him on making it back to Dry Creek alive. Either that or they felt they needed to acknowledge him before they loaded up one of the little plastic plates Angelina had brought for the food. He didn't mind, though. Just looking down the line he saw Pastor Matthew Curtis, and his wife, Glory. Then there was Sheriff Carl Wall again, and a woman that must be his wife. He hadn't realized he knew so many people in this small town until he saw them lined up like this. Maybe he had judged the people here too harshly. They seemed to welcome him.

Angelina walked into the kitchen and picked up some red oven mitts that she had brought with her from the Elkton ranch. Then she reached into the hot oven and pulled two metal sheets out that were piled high with quiche bites and stuffed mushrooms. The smell was tempting, and more than one person turned to look at the food as she carried it to the table where it would be served as a buffet. She'd put a thick covering over the wood table. The cold appetizers had already been set up along with pitchers filled with lemonade. Coffee was perking on the counter. The pastor had said a blessing for the food before they left the living room, so when Angelina set the platters on the table the children had already lined up.

Angelina had discovered the people in Dry Creek had a fair number of community meals and they always followed the same pattern. Special guests went first in line along with anyone who used a cane. Children second. The ladies next and then men.

"Tyler," she called softly.

She wasn't sure he would be able to hear her with everyone talking, but he seemed to sense her.

"Come get in line," she continued, using a hand gesture to make sure he knew he was entitled to eat first.

He shook his head. "I'll wait."

She almost walked over to him then. He looked a little shell-shocked. She knew it was a lot to take in.

But then the wave of people started and she was busy. She enjoyed feeding people and tonight was no exception. The contented sigh of a five-year-old boy as he bit into one of her stuffed mushrooms made her feel good. She was glad she had made the appetizers herself. She could have bought them, but they wouldn't have been the same. Sometimes, she reminded herself, having more money to use didn't give anyone a better outcome.

By the time the men were in line, Angelina had emptied all of the boxes she'd packed earlier. The platters were still loaded so she knew there would be enough and it was nice to see people have hearty appetites.

Angelina prayed as she worked tonight. The words Mrs. Hargrove had spoken gave her hope. She knew Tyler had not known much about God when he was her bodyguard in high school. She certainly had been no example back then, either, not that he would expect that because he must know she wasn't a Christian then. Maybe all Tyler needed was to hear some of the Gospel.

She saw Mrs. Hargrove go over to him as he stood at the end of the food line. She motioned for him to bend over and she whispered something in his left ear. He nodded.

Please, Lord, Angelina prayed. *Make Tyler's heart soft toward You. Give us all the words to encourage him.*

One of the cowboys went out on the porch and started to play his guitar. The sound filtered into the kitchen as the line of men finished passing by the food table. She smiled. She could already hear the murmur of approval as the ranch hands bit into the stuffed mushrooms. The house was crowded when everyone was standing so people started slipping outside. Angelina thought she just might follow now that almost everyone else had a plate.

She stepped easily outside and relaxed with her first glance around the yard. She was at peace in this place. She felt like she was among friends. She'd been in settings that were much more glamorous and yet she had been lonely. She wondered what it was about the people in Dry Creek that made her feel like she had a home here, even if it was only for a short time.

Chapter Six

A couple of hours had passed and everyone had taken their little plastic plates outside so they could look at the full moon. Tyler was sitting on the back of his pickup giving his knee a rest. He was walking better every day, but his leg still ached when he'd been on it too much. Besides, it was a good night to sit in the quiet and look at the stars. It was dark, but the temperature hadn't gone down much yet.

His mother had turned on the yard light, which stood out by the barn on the top of a high pole. It was old and weak, but it cast a golden glow without dimming the light of the night sky. The cowboys were leaning on the log corral posts by the barn, and some of the women were walking over by the lilac bushes. The chickens were cooped up for the night and Prince was playing tag with the Stone family dog.

The folks in Dry Creek knew how to party. Even Mrs. Hargrove's prayer had a celebratory feel to it. He wasn't quite sure what to think of the moment tonight when he felt a power surge toward God, but he suspected it was just the odd feeling of attending his own memorial service. Something like that was bound to make a man wonder about all kinds of things he'd never thought about before. He was hard-pressed to think God was paying that kind of attention to him anyway.

Tyler heard someone walking up from the other side of his vehicle and he turned. It was Wade. His brother had taken off his suit and changed into jeans and a flannel shirt.

"I've been sent to inform you that Saturday is date night at the café in Dry Creek," Wade said and lifted his hands up in a truce. "I know, I know, it's none of our business. But I'm just the messenger. My better half wanted me to tell you that. No pressure. But the owner, Linda Enger, brings in roses for the tables. And, if you call her tomorrow, she'll set you up a private corner."

"How private can it be?" Tyler felt bound to ask. He'd been in the café. "Unless she sets the table back in the kitchen."

"She has a Japanese screen," Wade said. "She puts it in the right corner by the kitchen door and it looks nice."

Tyler shrugged.

Wade sat down next to him then.

It was silent a minute before his brother got down to what he'd likely come to say. "You know, none of us boys have an easy time with trusting someone with our feelings."

"I—" Tyler figured it might be time for him to go mingle some. He started to slide forward. He might have experienced some strange feelings tonight, but he wasn't sure he wanted to talk about any of them.

Wade put his hand on Tyler's shoulder so he couldn't move any farther. "I'm just saying you aren't alone in feeling nervous about this kind of thing with Angelina."

Tyler looked around in a panic until he determined that she was not anywhere near. "Keep your voice down. Sound travels on a night like this with a full moon."

"That's just an old cowboy superstition."

"Still."

"All I'm saying is for you to think about it." Wade lowered his voice to a whisper. "Dating her."

"It's not that simple—"

"Yes, it is," his brother said, and then grinned.

"Angelina dated a different guy every week in high school."

"So, she was finding herself. Any of them serious?"

"Not that I ever heard."

"How about you?"

Tyler looked up. "How about me what?"

"Was there anyone you cared about back then, except for your Angelina, of course?"

Tyler shook his head. "I was busy working."

"A man in love finds time," Wade said with a smile.

"I don't know. High school was a long time ago. She might not want to date me now."

Wade appeared to consider that piece of information and then he said, "Well, this is your best shot at finding out. What kind of a woman would turn down a guy who asks for a date at his own memorial service? She has to say yes."

Tyler grunted. "I can't promise anything. I've never been husband material. And now with my arm injured the way it is, I'm even less so."

"It's just one date," Wade said then as he took his hand off Tyler's shoulder. "What could go wrong?"

With that Wade lifted himself off the pickup and walked away.

Tyler didn't even want to think about what could go wrong. But he had to admit he'd been watching Angelina as she walked in the yard, passing around the last of the quiches like she was circulating in some grand ballroom. She had interacted with his family and neighbors all evening as though they were no different than her usual friends. Maybe she had changed since high school.

No, he decided, Angelina had never been a snob. She'd been fickle though and that was the problem. She said she had changed, but he wasn't sure. Maybe Wade and his mother were right; maybe he should find out what kind of person Angelina was these days.

Suddenly, she turned and started walking straight toward him. He wondered if she had felt his eyes on her in the dark. He reached up to slick back his hair. He started pushing himself off the bed of the pickup so he would be standing. He winced when his weight came down on his legs. His jaws clenched in the pain.

"I saved the last quiche for you," Angelina said as she stepped close, and then lifted up the platter.

Tyler was silent as he waited for the spasm of pain to subside.

"That's very nice of you," he said when he could speak.

"Well, you are the guest of honor." She smiled. "And you've been a good sport about all the teasing. Although there wasn't as much as I expected."

"It's been kind of fun," Tyler said as he reached up and took the quiche. "I've never had a party for me before."

"Not even a birthday party?"

Tyler shook his head. "Mom used to bake us a cake, but we never had what you might call a party." He could see the sympathy well up in her blue eyes and he didn't want that. "A cake was good enough for me, though. After all, there are children starving in other countries. A cake would be a prize for them."

He scolded himself. They never had any visitors on the ranch except for their neighbors, the Mitchells. His father hadn't allowed it. But Tyler did not need to tell her that.

Angelina nodded like she wasn't convinced. She was still looking at him with concern so he figured he would never have a better time to get this said.

"Say—speaking of cake." He swallowed. He reminded himself that the words didn't need to be smooth, just coherent enough so she could understand them. "I was wondering if I could take you to the café for dinner tomorrow night. We could talk over old times and—"

"I'd love to," Angelina said, smiling. "I have to feed the ranch hands first, but I'd love to go with you."

Tyler nodded. "Good then. It's a date."

He wanted to be sure she knew that. He relaxed when she didn't seem alarmed.

"I finish putting supper on the table at the bunkhouse by six," she said.

"I'll be there to get you."

Just like that he had his first date in years. And then someone called to him from the house. "Tyler. The phone. It's for you."

"I'll be right back," Tyler said, looking toward the house. "Don't go away."

"I might just go over and talk to some people." She waved in the general direction of the ranch hands.

"Mrs. Hargrove might need some company." Tyler had followed some of those ranch hands and they had been looking at Angelina all night. He scowled at them now even though they couldn't see his face. He remembered she'd been holding the hand of that good-looking one during the prayer time. "You might tell Mrs. Hargrove that your father says he's coming in on Sunday. She has that room over her garage. I thought he might be able to stay there."

"My father?" Angelina gasped. "In a room over someone's garage?"

Just when Tyler started toward the house, he saw Angelina grin.

"That's perfect," she said and gave him a thumbs-up sign. "Absolutely perfect."

* * *

Angelina watched Tyler walk away, the grin growing wider on her face. Her father might have just been trying to rattle everyone with the possibility that he would come. But right now, she was happy either way. She looked around and the night seemed to get softer. Tyler had asked her out on a date. She felt like dancing. Or maybe not. Maybe this was one of those things a person wanted and then when they got it, it made more problems for them. Maybe there was a chance for them yet. She set her platter down and sat on the back of Tyler's pickup. The party would go on fine without her for a few minutes.

She lay back on the bed of the pickup and looked up at the stars. She could hardly believe she'd never really appreciated the stars until this summer. The steel was cold on her elbows as she leaned on them to rise up slightly so she could see over the side of the pickup. She supposed she had been too busy reaching for the glittery things around her to notice something as majestic as a summer sky until now.

She wondered if she would have healed from the pain of her mother's death more quickly in a place like this.

A noise made her look over near the barn and she saw Wade's wife, Amy, walking toward her, stepping carefully over the ruts in the yard. In the moonlight, the soft curve of her stomach showed her pregnancy.

"Wade told me I should wear my tennis shoes," Amy said as she came close enough to lean against the pickup.

She stood there a moment breathing hard. "But I told him I wasn't going to a party in my barn shoes."

"We didn't know we were going to end up outside." Angelina sat up and leaned over to pat the other woman's shoulder. "Do you want me to get you something?"

Amy shook her head. "I'm fine. Just breathing for two now." She smiled. "Everyone told me about the eating for two, but no one told me I'd be out of breath so much. Or maybe that just comes from overdoing the eating part."

Amy stopped to grin at her and then she continued. "I have to say, though, it's fun to come to a party like this and feel like I can eat as much as I want. Those appetizers you made are delicious."

"I could go get you some more," Angelina offered. "I saved a few in the oven."

Amy shook her head. "I just came over to tell you that it's been a wonderful memorial service."

"You're not leaving yet?"

"No, I just didn't want to forget to thank you."

They sat together for a moment, each lost in thought.

"I don't think we planned on people wanting to sit around and talk outside," Angelina finally said. "But I'm glad that's what's happening."

"And you have the best seat in the house." Amy used her arms to lift herself onto the back of the pickup, too.

Angelina helped the other woman to get settled. "Everyone looks like they're having a good time."

Amy nodded. "I'm glad you said that. I wondered

if you might think our parties aren't as grand as they ought to be. You know with the fancy chandeliers and stuff. Tuxedoes and caviar."

"What can compare with the night sky?" Angelina said, leaning back to get the full effect of the stars. "And congenial companions in blue jeans."

"I could name a few things," Amy said. "Broadway shows. Paris restaurants. You've lived quite a life before coming here for the summer."

Angelina sat back up so she could look at the other woman. "Dry Creek is nice."

Was it her imagination or did the other woman blush, Angelina wondered.

"Oh, I'm no good at this," Amy finally said, sounding exasperated. "I'm supposed to be the one coming over to tell you that we have the best place in the world to live right here. Jake kept saying I should emphasize that we have good water. And low pollution."

"Well, that sounds good."

"We have good men, too," Amy said. "The Stone men are the best you can find. They're loyal. Hard-working. They make good fathers. You should see Wade and Jake with Jake's daughter, Lara. They both let her pin up their hair if she's playing beautician."

"You're fortunate to have a husband and brother-in-law like that."

"They're good brothers to each other," Amy said, with an emphatic nod of her head. "And now with Tyler here, too. Wade's like an old mother hen, trying to get his last chick tucked in under his wing."

"I'm glad Tyler has brothers like that."

Amy nodded. "Tyler's a good man. Handsome, too."

Sometimes, Angelina thought, the trouble with a night sky was that it was easy to miss the things in front of you when your eyes were trained on the distance. She'd been sitting here listening to Amy and it reminded her that Wade had been over here talking to Tyler just like they were doing now.

"Wade didn't just tell Tyler to ask me out on a date, did he?"

"Why—" Amy gasped.

"It's okay," Angelina said, quickly. She slid down to the end of the pickup and stepped down to the ground. She had seen the guilt on the other woman's face. "I have to go check on Prince. He's probably chasing a chicken or something by now."

"The chickens are all in their coops and you're welcome to leave Prince here for the night."

"Well, I should see where he is anyway. And I wanted to check with Mrs. Hargrove about getting a ride back to where I left my car earlier today."

Angelina blinked several times as she walked away from the pickup. She would be okay. There were as many men out there to date as there were stars in the sky. She shouldn't even be surprised that someone had to twist Tyler's arm before he'd ask her out on a date. The only other time when she'd asked him about the two of them, and that had been years ago in high school, he had mumbled something about them not suiting. He had probably made his mind up about her way back then and there was no changing it now.

No wonder he didn't care if her father came here on Sunday or not. He figured his boss would stop them from having date number two anyway.

She saw Mrs. Hargrove finishing her walk by the lilac bushes.

"How are you, dear?" the older woman said as Angelina walked near.

"It's been a long night."

Mrs. Hargrove nodded, looking at her closely. "Charley and I are thinking of heading back home."

"Could I get a ride with you to where I left my car?" Angelina said, wrapping her arms around herself. It had suddenly gotten chilly. "I can pay you for gas."

"Nonsense," the other woman said as she put a hand on Angelina's shoulder. "It's been quite the day, hasn't it?"

Angelina nodded, not looking up to meet her friend's gaze.

"This was really nice what you did for Tyler," Mrs. Hargrove added.

"But I didn't do it for him," Angelina said, her eyes looking up of their own accord. "I mean, I thought this memorial service tonight would make everyone feel better, more settled, but he's not dead and—"

"I know," Mrs. Hargrove said, squeezing her shoulder. "It was easier when you didn't have to decide how to feel about him all over again."

Angelina stared into the face of the woman who had

become like a mother to her. "He's not a Christian, you know."

"I figure God hasn't had the last word on that yet."

"And I'm not sure he likes me."

"He likes you." The older woman started them walking toward the cars. "Don't fret about that. I've known Tyler since he was a boy and he has that look in his eyes when he's around you."

"It might just be heartburn," Angelina said with a smile. "He always used to tell me I gave him heartburn."

"Well, that's a start."

Mrs. Hargrove motioned to her husband who was standing over with some men by one of the pickups. Then he started toward their car, too.

"Men sometimes have a hard time sorting out their feelings," the older woman said. "The important thing is that they do have the emotions there to begin with."

Lord, Angelina prayed as they walked. *You know my heart. You know Tyler. Don't let me set myself up for being hurt.*

She looked back when they reached the Hargroves' car and she saw Tyler coming out of the house. Years ago, he'd been the one to greet her after her dates brought her home, even if he wasn't on duty that night. Not even her father bothered with that. It had taken Angelina some time to realize she enjoyed talking to him about her dates more than she did going on the dates themselves. She missed him.

She saw Prince go up to him then and nuzzle his leg until Tyler bent down to scratch behind the dog's ear.

Her dog and her old friend had bonded. Maybe she was
the one who didn't know how to make a relationship
stick. The two of them seemed to be doing fine. She
was the one on the outside again.

Chapter Seven

Saturday went by too fast and before he knew it Tyler was walking slowly across the yard of the Elkton ranch to pick Angelina up for their date. The sun was setting, but he could see well enough. He'd had to park by the main gate and was now walking over to the bunkhouse. He was limping more than usual and he stopped once to adjust his tie while holding a bouquet of roses in the same hand. Unfortunately, his left hand wasn't closing any better today than it had been and was useless for either task.

He felt like a boy on his first date. His mother had insisted on ironing a shirt for him although he assured her he could handle it. Wade had brought over some woodsy cologne that he wanted Tyler to try because Amy said any woman would fall at his feet when she smelled it. Jake had come by then to shake his head, muttering something about fools, before he went out to his pickup and brought back this bouquet of long-stem red roses wrapped in gold lace paper with a white plastic heart stuck in the middle of it for no good reason except sentiment.

Tyler had tried to stop the flow of help, protesting that he knew how to dress himself for a date. He could buy his own flowers and chose his own cologne. Finally, he had to grit his teeth so he didn't say anything that would hurt his family. He wasn't used to accepting help from anyone. The truth was, he believed a man had to be able to make it on his own in this life and he didn't know what to do with all their offers of assistance.

One thing he had learned at his memorial service was that he shouldn't push people away when they wanted to come closer. He had prided himself for a long time on not needing anyone else, but when a man faced his death that solitude was not particularly comforting. He wished whoever had sent him that wreath would come up and tell him so he could repay him or her and be done with it. The thought of having an unknown friend like that was making him look at everyone differently since he didn't know which one had been the giver.

He had gotten a call from Clyde a few hours ago and Tyler was going to need to talk business with Angelina tonight, too. He had made arrangements for their date at the café so he hoped to get the talk about the investigation on Angelina's father out of the way before they even ordered their meal. That would be one nice thing about the screen around their table. No one could eavesdrop on what he had to say.

Tyler was so preoccupied that he was halfway to the bunkhouse before he stopped and looked around. The barn was to his left and he recognized the smells in the corral—last year's alfalfa hay and horses. He hadn't realized how much he missed ranching, especially the sounds of the animals, until now.

There was more green grass on the ground here than he'd seen in town. Someone was watering the soil regularly and had probably spread fertilizer in the spring. He'd been on this ranch several times as a boy and he could see signs of progress. A dozen new pickups, all four-wheel-drive, were lined up on the west side of the barn, ready for the cowboys to use when they went out to check the miles of barbed wire fence that marked off the acreage. A new tractor, with a glassed-in cab, was pulled up next to the other vehicles. A black three-wheeler was there, too, for small jobs.

It was good to know a Montana ranch could be prosperous if people worked at it, he thought as he saw the bunkhouse come into view. The building had wood shingles on the side of it, stained brown to blend in with the trees that had been planted around it. To the right was a smaller building that he'd guess was the kitchen and cook's quarters. Everything around was well tended, including the porches leading up to the buildings.

Tyler had not talked with his brothers any further about partnering with them on the Stone family ranch, but he was worried they would coddle him if he did. They still thought of him as their baby brother and his injuries worried them. He couldn't take the offer if they were going to be helping him do his part all the time. It wouldn't be fair. A man needed to pull his own weight. It was a pity though. He'd woken up this morning, staring at the ceiling in the bedroom he'd known as a boy, and looked out the window to the fields. He had dressed quickly and tiptoed down the stairs so he wouldn't wake his mother. Then he'd walked out to the nearest field, bent down and rolled some soil through his fingers. He could feel the call of the land going through him just like it had his father before him.

Maybe he could save up enough to buy his own ranch around here somewhere. Even if he wasn't sure about getting involved with the neighbors, there was something about the land around Dry Creek that made him want to stay. He supposed it was the pull of the Stone family history. There was no rule that a man needed to join in with the social life of the small community just because he lived in the area.

He wouldn't mind being closer to his family, either, he admitted to himself as he pulled his mind back to the present and started up the steps to the bunkhouse. If they could stop themselves from helping him then it would be okay. Well, except for whatever secret their mother was holding back from him. His brothers hadn't even given him a hint when he asked today. They'd just said their mother would tell him when she was ready.

When Tyler stood in front of the solid wood door of the bunkhouse, he realized he should have planned better. It was obvious from the amount of noise coming from inside that the ranch hands were just sitting down to supper. He had hoped to get Angelina away without seeing any of the cowboys. Although they had curbed their teasing last night, he didn't expect their truce to extend much longer.

But, he told himself as he raised his hand to knock, there was nothing else he could do now but forge ahead and hope for the best.

The silence that greeted his knock was almost worse than the noise that had preceded it. He realized most of the men probably didn't knock when they entered. Likely most of their guests didn't, either. He'd just marked himself as a stranger.

Angelina opened the door for him, and his heart skipped a beat. She was a vision. She wore a white sundress with straps that tied behind her neck and a beaded red necklace hanging down. Her arms and face were a golden tan and, with her long hair touching her shoulders, she was breathtaking.

"I'll be just a minute," she said, looking nervous. "I have the food on the table, but I wanted to grab another pan of biscuits from the kitchen."

"I'll go with you." The kitchen building was right across a small walkway from the bunkhouse.

"Hey, Tyler," a voice called from inside the latter. "Come on in and sit a minute."

"They won't give up until you do," Angelina said with a grin as she started walking. "I'll be right back."

"Here, take these with you." Tyler took a few steps so he could hand her the flowers. "The men will eat me alive if I take them inside."

"They're lovely," Angelina said as she stopped, turned and took the bouquet a little shyly.

She looked up at him then and Tyler stepped closer. "They're not as lovely as you."

That wasn't very original, he knew, but Angelina blushed and he forgot about impressing her. He reached up a hand to touch her cheek.

"Quite lovely," he added.

The pink on her skin gave her a delicate appearance. And her eyes looked suddenly vulnerable as they met his. They stood there in silence.

"I still need to fix my hair," Angelina finally said as she pulled away and put her hand up to pat a few strands back into place. "I'm running late, but I'll be quick."

"I'll be here when you're ready."

She nodded, and then turned and hurried toward the other building.

Tyler sighed. He wondered if he was going to survive tonight. A voice in his head kept cautioning him that Angelina was only playing at her life right now. It was hard to believe that her years of living in luxury could be shrugged off as casually as she seemed to believe. She'd been raised to have servants, not to serve others. He just couldn't believe she was happy cooking for a bunch of cowboys on the ranch here and then going out to eat with him in a country diner that had probably never served crème brûlée in all the years it had been in business.

Tyler turned his face back to the bunkhouse. He wasn't sure he was ready for the teasing, but he figured he could stand almost anything if Angelina was coming back soon. So he stepped up to the open door and walked inside. He smelled the roast beef before he looked close at the long wood table that stood in the middle of the room. A dozen men were sitting there with empty white plates in front of them and big bowls of mashed potatoes and gravy on the table along with the platter of meat and a bowl of green beans.

Whether Angelina was born to this life or not, she seemed to be doing a good job cooking for the ranch hands.

"Don't let me keep you from eating," Tyler said as he made his way over to the sofa. He hoped to savor the closeness he'd felt with Angelina a little longer.

"We can't eat until all of the biscuits are here anyway," a red-haired man said as the rest of the cowboys looked over and examined Tyler like he was the most interesting person to have sat on that sofa all day. It made him want to reach up and adjust his tie just in case it was crooked.

It was silent for a minute. And then he looked down at the coffee table in front of the sofa. A few horse magazines lay on top of some flyers.

"There aren't enough biscuits to go around at two a piece." Finally, another man offered a bit of conversation. "Besides, Calen isn't here yet. He had to drop something off at the main house."

"So you wait for him?" Tyler asked absentmindedly. Something about the corner of the yellow flyer looked familiar. He moved one of the magazines.

"Five minutes," several of the ranch hands said in unison and then one of them added, "Two more to go."

They were silent after that and Tyler was preoccupied with the flyer. It was from the same florist who had brought Angelina's flowers and the wreath out to the house yesterday. He remembered the logo on those two delivery receipts he'd signed.

"We had a good time at your memorial service last night," a man with a beard said. "Nice of you to invite us."

"Glad you came," Tyler said, looking up and trying to be as cordial as he could. "And thanks for not giving me too hard of a time."

"You can thank him," the man nodded as the door opened and Calen stepped inside. "He said we were to take it easy on you. Said you were almost blown up in a bomb in Afghanistan and that was enough for any man."

"He said that, did he?" Tyler stood up. He rubbed his neck to lessen the tension in his muscles. The flyer didn't mean anything. Angelina must have left it there. Maybe she had sat at the sofa when she ordered those big bowls of wildflowers.

Just then Angelina came through the door. She'd pulled her blond hair up and tucked one of his roses into it somehow. She was so beautiful he forgot all about flowers. She held a baking sheet heaped with biscuits in one hand and her purse in the other.

"I'll do the dishes when I get back," she said to the men as she put the metal sheet on the table. "But I'd like you to take your plates and everything across to the sink."

"I'll see it gets done." Calen looked at Tyler and then Angelina with a fondness Tyler hadn't expected. "Have fun now."

"Try and stop us," Tyler said as they both walked toward the door.

He never had been much for dating, Tyler thought to himself as he held the door open for Angelina, but he was going to make up for that tonight. He wanted to dazzle Angelina.

"Have her back by midnight," one of the men called after them and the rest of them laughed.

The door slammed shut behind them and they walked down the stairs.

"Well, that wasn't bad," Tyler said. The sun had started to set in earnest now and before long it would be dusk.

"No," she agreed.

They hadn't taken two steps before Tyler's curiosity overcame him and he stopped to turn toward her. "Did you order the wildflowers off that yellow flyer I just saw on the coffee table?"

She shook her head. "I went to the shop in Miles City to do it. I wanted to see what they looked like first. I may have left the flyer in the bunkhouse someplace, but I didn't use it. Why?"

"I'm just wondering who ordered that big wreath," he said. "I'd like to pay them back for it if I can find them. Not many people around here can afford that kind of thing."

Angelina shrugged her shoulders. "They obviously decided they could. Can't someone just do something nice for you?"

"I know I should be more open to help," he finally admitted. "It's probably not healthy that I can't. I mean I know women like the men they date to be more—you know—sensitive."

He forgot all about dazzling Angelina and began to just hope he'd survive the dinner without putting her completely off him. And then she smiled and all was well.

"Maybe you just need some practice," she said as she reached over and took his right hand. Fortunately, that was his good one.

With that simple gesture, he figured she was going to forgive him for his failings. Which was a good thing because he appeared to have more than a few. And he didn't know how to give up his desire to be independent. In his mind, a man needed to be a man.

They walked together back to the pickup. This time Tyler didn't think about the condition of the soil under his feet or the animals out in the barn. The sun was setting more deeply and the landscape had turned rosy from the red sky in the west. His heart started to beat a little faster as it turned to romance.

Angelina was surprised when Tyler walked over to a new beige pickup. "What happened to the black one?"

The pickup was parked next to the wood rail fence that marked off the drive to the main house. None of the Elkton family had lived in that house for months but the yard was kept nicely and the fence recently painted white. Angelina knew that the cowboys in the bunkhouse worried Garth and Sylvia Elkton might sell the ranch if they could find a buyer. The couple was spending most of their time in Seattle running a camp for disadvantaged youth and Garth's son was some highpowered politician in Washington, D.C. Angelina figured the house would stand empty for a long time if no one bought it.

"Wade lent me his pickup for tonight," Tyler said as he opened the passenger door for her. "He's got the deluxe model."

"Oh," Angelina said as she climbed into the cab and settled herself. The seats were soft ivory leather and mini-speakers were built into both doors. Gold trim outlined the steering wheel and everything still smelled new.

She looked over at Tyler as he stood by her open door. "I kind of like the old one."

"Really?" Tyler said skeptically. "It's pretty beat up."

He leaned one arm on the frame of the door.

She nodded. It was growing darker, but she could still see his eyes. "Your pickup wasn't too old when you used to take me places in it. I liked that."

"We went in my pickup only when the chauffeur got sick," Tyler said, a smile softening his face. "We had to call it in as an emergency so your father didn't have a heart attack. He used to call my pickup a glorified tin can."

"It was my wonderful chariot when I needed a ride home from the prom, though."

She'd never forget that night. She'd been stood up in the most public way by her date. If Tyler hadn't stepped on to the dance floor and made it look like she'd planned to waltz with him all along, she would have been humiliated as only a teenager could be. By the time they needed to go home though she had completely forgotten about the miserable guy she'd had the misfortune to come with. Tyler had told her story after story about Dry Creek all night long. They'd laughed and talked and she'd rested her head against his shoulder. She'd wished with all her heart that he'd been her real date for the evening.

"I still think you should have let me go back and punch that Ricky Hanes for you."

"You remember his name?"

"Of course, I remember. I was going to give him a tongue lashing he'd never forget, too."

She shook her head. "I didn't want you to leave me. And my heart wasn't broken. I found out later he was trying to make me jealous by going off and dancing with that other girl. But it backfired. I had a good time without him." She leaned closer to tell him the rest. "Some of my girl friends called me the next day and said you were the best-looking guy at the prom. Tall, dark and handsome. And you had that inscrutable look on your face. Very mysterious."

"I was probably just concentrating on counting out my steps. I'd never been to something like that before. I had to borrow a tuxedo from one of the other bodyguards so I could blend in—and that was when I didn't plan on dancing."

"The prom was one of the few times when there wasn't a plan," she said as she moved back a little so she was sitting straight on the seat again.

He nodded.

She leaned back. "I never thought I would survive all the coordination it took to do even the most basic things like get to school on time."

Every move she made her senior year in high school had been choreographed by the security detail. If she wanted to go shopping with a friend, she needed to give them two hours notice.

"I used a flowchart. A different color for each day of the week so I'd keep them straight," Tyler said.

"I remember. Friday was hot pink on the chart. I always thought that was so romantic."

Tyler laughed. "I picked pink because it is the color of those antacids. Fridays were always a challenge because that's when you had your dates."

And with that, he closed the door gently and walked around to the other side of the pickup so he could get in the driver's side.

Tyler turned on the headlights and checked all of his mirrors. She remembered he'd always been careful. It used to annoy her. She was too impatient. Now she saw it as him making sure of their safety.

"I'm glad we're finally going out on a date together," she whispered in the growing darkness.

"Me, too." His voice was almost as soft as hers.

They were both silent for a moment after that.

Then Tyler put the car in gear and started the pickup.

She had no expectations for tonight. No master plan. But, looking over at the smile flitting across Tyler's face, she did know that whatever happened tonight she would never forget it.

Chapter Eight

Wispy clouds were covering part of the moon as Tyler drove his brother's pickup down the road into Dry Creek. Angelina was quiet as she sat in the passenger seat. Tyler had also been silent, putting most of his energy into stopping himself from reaching over to the other side of the seat and taking one of her hands in his. He knew his left hand wasn't up to controlling the steering wheel by itself, though, and he wasn't so sure his heart would thank him for holding her hand, either. He needed to remember that this evening was all about the past in Angelina's mind. They were not building a future; they were saying goodbye to dreams they used to have. And holding someone's hand brought to mind couples who were going to spend the rest of their lives together. Those fantasies were not for him. Besides, Angelina would forget about him once she went back home.

Tyler parked the pickup and took out the ignition key.

Angelina turned to look at him then, uncertainty in her eyes. Without thought, he reached over with his good hand and touched Angelina on the cheek. He opened his hand and she nestled the side of her face against it. Her pulse fluttered against the bottom of his thumb.

"I forgot to tell you I quit my job with your father," he whispered.

She turned to him then with a laugh, deep and throaty. "I doubt he agrees that you're done."

Angelina's skin was petal soft and he ran his thumb across her cheekbone. A faint yellow light came through the windshield from the single bulb on the café porch. It made her tanned face look golden in the darkness.

"I just didn't want you to think I would—well, if I still was employed as your bodyguard I wouldn't—that is, I wouldn't speak of—"

Her blue eyes opened wider then. They were dark as the midnight sky and she looked at him as if he knew how to reach up into that sky and pull down a star. Then her lip trembled ever so slightly. He had no choice but to give voice to what had been welling up inside of him ever since he'd met her.

"You are the most beautiful woman I have ever known," he whispered as he leaned close. "And I—" Now was the time, but he couldn't continue. "I value you highly."

There was scarcely room for breath between them, and he touched her lips lightly. He knew he had stumbled. He hadn't said enough. But he didn't know what he felt except for regret that he didn't have anything more to offer her. He decided to try again, but the glare of headlights shone in the side window.

A double cab pickup pulled up next to them and rowdy laughter spilled out into the night as the front and back doors opened. A radio was blaring and someone banged their hand on the hood of Wade's pickup, startling Angelina. The four men who stood there all wore Stetsons, dark jackets and boots.

Angelina frowned then as she bent forward and peered through the windshield. "I think those men are from the Elkton ranch. It looks like Ray, Glenn—I can't see their faces, but they shouldn't be here. I just fed them beef stew and biscuits a half hour ago."

Tyler clenched his jaw. "I doubt they're here because they're hungry."

She looked up at him.

"I think we have some chaperones for the evening," Tyler added as he watched the men open the door to the café and stomp inside.

"I don't think they should be—"

"It'll be fine," Tyler said, willing his muscles to relax. "The men will probably leave after they've each had a piece of pie. Especially if I pay for it."

Angelina shook her head. "I baked them pie two days ago. That should be enough for any man. They're going to have to start watching their cholesterol if they're not careful."

"I'll mention that to them," Tyler said as he unlatched his door.

Then he walked around to the other side of the pickup and opened the door for Angelina.

"Do you think we should say hello to them?" she asked as Tyler helped her down.

"It's up to you," Tyler replied as they stood close together, sheltered by the door. Neither one of them moved. "They can't exactly hide from us, though."

The door protected them from view and Tyler didn't want to go anywhere. He smelled Angelina's perfume, a sweet floral scent. Wayward strands of blond hair had fallen down from the clasp she wore in the back. Her shoulders were bare except for the straps of the sundress that tied behind her neck. As they stood there, the clouds overhead parted and, in the dark of the night, the moon shone down upon them fully.

"We've been blessed by God," Angelina said as she looked upward. "Yesterday I thought you were dead and now, here we are in the moonlight."

With that, she laid her face against his chest and he put his arms around her.

Tyler didn't know what to say. He wasn't so sure God had anything to do with them standing together here tonight, but he didn't want to say anything. Not now.

"Maybe you should give those men their pie to go," Angelina murmured then, her voice muffled against his shirt. "I don't want them coming over to borrow a saltshaker or something. Not when you're finally talking to me."

Tyler chuckled as he smoothed her hair back from her face. "We're supposed to have the date package so I think we get a screen of some kind."

"That better work," Angelina said as she looked up

at him. "Sometimes there are too many people around here who don't mind their own business. Maybe we should have a No Trespassing sign at our table, too."

"It's not like the East Coast," Tyler agreed and turned to offer her his arm. "No one just walks on by when they can stop and say hello."

Together they walked over to the porch steps and climbed them. Tyler opened the door and ushered Angelina into the café. There had been other pickups parked outside so he wasn't surprised to see that quite a few of the tables had been occupied before the cowboys came inside. The other diners looked like ranching couples, but he didn't recognize them.

Everyone in the place turned to look at them when they stepped inside. Except for the Elkton ranch hands.

"Excuse me a minute," Tyler whispered to Angelina.

Then he walked over to the cowboys' table. By the time he got there, every one of the four men had a menu in front of their face. Tyler had to appreciate that they'd slicked up for their trip here—everyone's hair was combed and they were all freshly shaven. He was quite sure they'd eaten their full share of biscuits and stew before leaving the bunkhouse. They must have driven quite a bit faster than he had down that gravel road for them to arrive so soon after he and Angelina did.

Tyler pulled over a chair from another table and straddled it backward. "I suppose you fellas have come to town for a piece of pie."

None of the menus were lowered, not even the one that was upside down.

"I'd be happy to buy each of you some pie," he continued, trying to make his voice as friendly as possible. "Apple. Cherry. Custard. Whatever they have."

Half of the menus came down with that.

The cowboys looked at each other and finally one of them asked, "Why would you do that?"

Tyler shrugged. "Just being neighborly."

"Well, that's real nice of you. If there's ever anything, we can—" The man's voice trailed off.

"As a matter of fact," Tyler said, "there is something you can do for me."

All of the menus were down by now.

"I suppose you want us to leave," one of the men said.

"Well, I want you to enjoy your pie first." Tyler stood up. "But I'm willing to pay for some ice cream to go with it if you promise to be done here in five minutes."

"We can't eat it in five minutes," the man protested. "The ice cream is too cold for that. We'd get—what is it—the freezing inside the mouth."

"Ten minutes then," Tyler said. "Fifteen minutes maximum. But no one comes over to our table to borrow the salt. Or the ketchup. Not so much as a toothpick."

"Nobody needs any of those things to eat their pie," the man concluded as he looked around at his fellow ranch hands. One by one, they nodded.

"We just got to thinking after you left," the man continued speaking. "You might be some kind of a hero on account of that bomb and all, but we don't know you really. And you Stone men always did have a reputation with the ladies. We don't want anyone to give our Angie any trouble."

"Her name's Angelina. Angelina Brighton."

"Well, there's no need to be touchy. We're just looking out for our own."

"I know," Tyler said, swallowing back his irritation. He'd known that all along. He might not like that they didn't trust him, but he couldn't fault them for caring about Angelina.

"I'd never hurt her," he told them quietly as he stood there. "I promise."

Four pairs of eyes measured his sincerity and finally the men gave reluctant nods.

"So eat your pie in peace," he said.

Then Tyler walked back to where Angelina stood.

"I never checked to see if they had pie on the menu tonight," he said suddenly after he stood a minute just inside the door.

"Those men don't need pie anyway. Maybe they can get a nice garden salad instead," Angelina suggested.

"I'm not going back and telling them that."

"They would thank you when they go to see their doctors." Angelina was a good five inches shorter than him so she had to look up to make eye contact. "But you don't need to worry. They always have pie here."

When she tipped her head up like that, Tyler had a hard time seeing anything more than her lips. She had some kind of a pink gloss on them that made them shimmer in what little light came from the overhead bulbs. The café was filled with soft shadows. Maybe the owner did something different on date night. He never remembered it looking like this in the daylight.

Tyler gave himself a mental shake. He didn't want to give Angelina's protectors any reason for concern or they'd be here before they even got their pie. He'd wait to say all he had to say until he and Angelina were seated. Maybe by then he'd think of the right way to say it.

He looked around. The café owner, Linda, must be in the kitchen. He could hear a radio playing softly in the back room and a strip of bright light showed from underneath the closed door.

He glanced down again and noticed the relaxed look on Angelina's face. He figured they were in no hurry to be seated.

"A person would think they were in some kind of a fifties movie here," he said. "Just standing in this place."

The linoleum on the floor was a black-and-white-checkered pattern and the wood tables scattered around had white tablecloths covering them. A single red rose sat in a vase in the middle of each table. It was a classy place Tyler decided. The walls were painted ivory and memorabilia was hanging here and there. He recognized some of it.

"I think that old guitar belongs to Duane Enger. You've heard of him?"

Angelina nodded. "I have some of his songs. And I think he was up for some music award last year. But mostly people here know him as Linda's husband. He doesn't take his tour bus out as often now that she's—" Angelina lowered her voice and looked around before finishing her statement "—she's expecting, but I don't know who she's told so be sure and keep it quiet."

Tyler grinned. "I'm guessing that means the whole town of Dry Creek knows by now."

Angelina nodded with a smile. "Maybe. Good news always travels fast around here."

"I guess that's just the kind of town it is."

"It's because the townspeople care," she agreed.

For the first time since he left, Tyler wondered if he had misjudged the hearts of people here. Maybe the people in the houses ten years ago hadn't shared any gossip with the news crews. Or, maybe if they had, they thought they were helping his mother.

Just then the door from the back room opened and Linda stepped out carrying two platters of food. She had on a white chef apron over a T-shirt and some blue jeans so she couldn't be too far along in her pregnancy. Her face did have a certain glow, though.

"Give me a minute," Linda said, giving Tyler and Angelina a nod.

Then she sat the platters down at a table and pulled a squeeze bottle of ketchup out of one of the big pockets on her apron. She pulled another bottle of mustard out of the other pocket. Then she unclipped an order pad from the waist of the apron and started walking over to where they stood.

"Could you get some pie for our friends there first?" Tyler said with a nod to the table with the Elkton ranch hands. "Just add it to my bill. And give them some ice cream for their pie if they want it."

"I'll take you to your table first." Linda motioned for them to follow her over to a corner table. Tyler hadn't noticed the black screen that leaned against the wall until they reached their destination.

"I'll just set this up for you," Linda said as she reached for the folded screen.

"Let me," Tyler said, stepping over to the screen himself and grabbing hold of it before she could.

Linda put her hands on her hips. "You're the customer. I'm supposed to be moving around the screen."

"No problem," Tyler said as he lifted the screen. "Where do you want it?"

"Right here," Linda said, pointing to a faint line on the floor, and then shaking her head. "I suppose you know about my secret. It seems everyone does. I'm surprised folks let me keep lifting the coffeepot."

Tyler set the screen where she wanted it.

"Nothing wrong with people caring about you," Tyler said then, surprised that the words would be coming out of his mouth. Maybe almost dying had changed the way he saw things.

Angelina beamed and he felt like he'd said something important.

Linda smiled. "Thank you for reminding me. Please, have a seat and I'll go get the order for your friends."

Tyler nodded as Linda stepped around the screen. Then he walked over and pulled out one of the chairs for Angelina. When she sat down, he pushed her chair in a little so that she was comfortable at the round table.

"Thank you," she said softly.

He went over to the other chair and seated himself.

Tyler could hear the murmur of voices as the ranch hands ordered their pie. In a few minutes, Linda was back on their side of the screen.

"That was easy," Linda reported. "We only have apple and blueberry at the moment. And they all wanted plain vanilla ice cream with it. Two scoops."

She unfolded her order pad. "The special tonight is a grilled pork chop with onions, creamed spinach and a baked sweet potato. Or you can have a burger any way you like—deluxe or plain. And we have an assortment of sandwiches and soup. You already know what we have for pie, but I also offer a fruit dessert plate."

Tyler lifted his eyebrow in a silent question to Angelina.

"The special sounds wonderful," she said. "With the fruit for after."

"Make it two," Tyler added.

With a promise to bring some ice water and fresh-baked rolls, Linda left to go get the pie for the ranch hands.

"Before we eat," Tyler said. "I thought I should let you know I got a call back from Clyde."

"What did he tell you?" Angelina asked, leaning forward.

"First, your Derrick seems to be above reproach," Tyler said a little ruefully. He'd rather hoped otherwise. "Apparently, he is a successful attorney with a good reputation. His business is solid and he has been collecting artwork lately."

"Artwork?"

Tyler nodded. "Some fairly nice pieces, according to Clyde. It seems he's doing some remodeling on a house he just recently purchased in hopes of getting married, so he's buying furnishings. Oh, and he's made several large donations to a mission in downtown Boston, so he's generous, too."

Tyler stopped to let the words sink in for Angelina.

"So he does want to get married?" she asked with a frown.

"It appears so."

"And my father? What did Clyde find out about him?"

Tyler wished he could wait to answer that until Clyde had more time to investigate, but he owed her a report just like he would anyone else. "Clyde says your father is putting out feelers about selling a couple of his businesses."

"Oh, he'd never do that," Angelina protested. "His businesses are more important to him than anything. I don't think he'd ever let them go. Maybe it's just something he's doing to try to make the company's stock go up or down. I've known him to do things like that."

"Well, you could be right," Tyler conceded. He wondered if Angelina knew that was illegal, and then decided it wasn't the point of tonight. "Clyde seemed to think the sales rumors were true, but he didn't get any sense that a deal has been made so it could be all smoke and mirrors."

Angelina sat there for a moment, with her forehead furrowed in thought.

Tyler continued. "The other piece of news that Clyde managed to dig up is about your father putting one of his houses on the market. The one you used to call your summer home."

"The Long Island place?" Angelina asked in surprise. "I always loved that house."

"I've never known your father to make a bad business decision so I'm not sure why he's doing any of this, but I expect he has his reasons."

"Is he giving any money to some charity, like Derrick is?"

"I don't know."

Angelina nodded. "Someone else could be blackmailing him even if Derrick isn't."

Just then Linda came back and set the bread and the water on the table before pulling out a lighter from her apron pocket. She leaned in then and lit the small candle on the table.

Tyler shook his head when they were alone again.

"Men like your father have too many people around them to be easily blackmailed," he assured her. "He has accountants and Mrs. Stevenson. He couldn't just take a million dollars out of his accounts without someone else knowing about it."

"Maybe they do know," Angelina said. "Last time I was back there I kept getting the impression that everyone knew a secret they weren't supposed to tell me."

Tyler shrugged. "I'll tell Clyde to look in to that angle

some more. But I wouldn't worry. There could be lots of things he might keep a secret that are harmless. Maybe he's getting you something for your birthday. Or maybe he's asked a woman out on a date and he doesn't want you to know."

"But I should know," Angelina protested.

"Just like he knows about all of your dates," Tyler replied, teasing her.

"Well, that's different, and you know it."

He smiled at that. He was grateful that her worries about her father were so different than his fears had been about Buck Stone. Wade and Jake seemed to have overcome the problems inherited from their abusive father, but Tyler wasn't sure he would be able to do the same. And, until he knew the answer to that question, he had no right feeling anything for someone like Angelina.

Angelina was waiting for the ranch hands to leave. She couldn't see through the screen so she didn't know if they were still there for sure, but she kept hearing the sounds of boots shuffling around under some table. Having the ranch hands here brought her back to high school and the days when it seemed she never went anywhere without a crowd of security personnel following her.

She glanced over at Tyler. He was studying his fork and she smiled.

"I admire you, you know," Angelina said.

He looked up at that.

"When I was twelve," she continued, "I was surrounded by enrichment programs and butlers. I don't think I even realized I was fortunate, though. I had never given anything to anyone. Oh, I may have given money to some cause, but I can't imagine I did anything like you did when you gave your coat to your mother."

"She needed it," Tyler said curtly. "It was cold."

"Still," Angelina said as she lifted her water glass, "it was impressive."

"She made too big of a thing of it last night," Tyler said, his voice flat.

Angelina took a drink of water and then said, "I don't think so."

Tyler's face tightened.

"It was my fault," he finally said, suppressed fury giving his voice an edge. "That's why I gave her the coat. If I had acted like a man, she never would have been taken off to prison."

"What do you mean?" Angelina had never seen Tyler this angry and it all seemed turned on himself.

"My father was mad at me that day in the barn," Tyler said, his eyes finally meeting hers. They flashed black, all of the warm brown gone. "If I had opened the door and gone inside, he and my mother wouldn't have kept going with their argument and she never would have killed him."

"Oh." Angelina put her hand out to cover his. "No one's told you yet. I'm so sorry."

"Told me what?"

"I just assumed your mother would want to be the one to tell you."

"She's keeping some secret from me, but she keeps saying that the time isn't right. At first I thought Wade and Jake both knew what it was, but lately I haven't been so sure. Whatever it is, she's waiting for what she thinks is the right moment."

Angelina frowned. "But that doesn't make any sense. Everyone knows."

Tyler's eyes demanded answers.

"Your mother didn't kill your father," Angelina said. "It turns out it was Mr. Mitchell, Amy's grandfather."

Tyler looked at her in disbelief. "Why would he do that? My whole family always got along with the Mitchells. They were the only people we ever had over to our place."

Angelina swallowed. "Apparently, your father got along too well with Amy's Aunt Tilly, Mr. Mitchell's daughter. They were having an affair and when the old man found out he went to your father to demand he call a halt to it. Evidently, your father told him to go on home and mind his own business. They may have had more words. But, in the end, Mr. Mitchell is the one who lifted up that shovel and brought it down on your father's head."

Tyler just stared at her. By this time, his face was pale even in the light of the small candle on their table.

"You mean it had nothing to do with me?" he asked.

"I don't think so," Angelina said gently.

He was quiet then and it was becoming clear to her that he'd just confided in her in a way he hadn't before. She knew it was hard for him to talk about his feelings.

"I'm sure your mother will tell you the same thing."

Just then Linda stepped around the corner of the screen carrying two plates of food.

"Smells delicious," Angelina said, trying to give Tyler some time before he had to speak. She tried to hide her relief. If Tyler would only talk to her about how he felt, their whole relationship would change. He would see she'd become an adult. He would trust her. They'd have a chance at something.

Linda put the plates down in front of them. "Anyone want some ground pepper?"

"Sure," Tyler said, and she pulled a wooden pepper grinder out of her apron pocket.

"How about you?" Linda asked her.

"Yes, please," Angelina answered.

With that, Linda ground pepper over their plates. When she finished, she walked away from their table.

"I guess that's shocking news about your father," Angelina said, just in case Tyler wanted to talk about it even more.

"You can say that again." Tyler picked up his fork, and then put it back down again like he didn't know what to do. "I suppose you want us to say a blessing before we eat."

It wasn't a question, Angelina thought, but she nodded anyway. "Please."

"I don't usually pray," Tyler said. "Just wanted you to know. I am grateful, though, even if I don't say the words."

"I think the words are important," she said. "But they don't have to be fancy."

Tyler nodded at that and bowed his head. Then he opened them again and looked up. "Do we get to hold hands when we pray?"

He looked so eager she grinned. "If you want."

Tyler held his right hand out, leaving his injured one lying next to his plate.

She reached out both hands to him, though. At first, she thought he wasn't going to connect with both hands, but he finally held out his injured hand, too.

"I'll be careful with it," she said as she took his right hand, and then gently held his left one as well.

Angelina bowed her head when she had both of his hands. She felt connected to him and was willing to wait for him to feel comfortable, too.

"God," Tyler said abruptly, his head bowed, "I know I should have been saying thanks for some time now, but I figure You'll be listening to Angelina's prayers and I can kind of piggyback to get word to You that I'm grateful. I know we don't have much to do with each other, but I figure I owe You. That's about all I have to say, but I just wanted You to know that."

"Amen," Angelina said as Tyler ended his prayer. She looked up and saw that he was looking puzzled.

"Did you feel that?" he asked. "Some kind of electrical short running through the floor or something?"

Angelina looked down. "I don't think that's possible. It's tile here."

"It must be me then." Tyler shook his head. "I shouldn't be saying any prayers."

"Why ever not?"

"Well, for one thing, I don't know that God is up there listening to anyone—and, if He is, I'm pretty sure He's not listening to me."

Angelina didn't think it was a good time to tell him how many people around here were still praying for him.

"I can see why you'd want to study on it," she said instead. "No place better to do that than in church tomorrow morning. Why don't you come?"

"Herc? In Dry Creek?"

"I expect your mother and brothers will be going."

Angelina almost had pity on him. He looked drawn and hunted.

"It would mean a lot to me if you would come," she finally said.

Tyler looked even more cornered, but he did nod. "I guess you're right. I should check it out and see what is happening there."

"So you can report to my father?" Angelina asked, all of the hope draining out of her.

"No," he protested, his eyes flashing. "I would check it out because it's important to you. If it means so much to you—making you agree to serve as camp cook for the bunkhouse crew—I know it has to be important."

Angelina's hope soared. "It's not just a phase, you know. I've grown up. I don't flit from thing to thing like I did in high school."

Tyler nodded, his eyes measuring her.

"You can trust me," she whispered. "I know what my feelings are. They're not going to go away tomorrow because some new and exciting thing happens. I'm working really hard to be committed to people. I'm trying to live like the Bible says. Letting my yes be yes and my no be no. I want to honor my father. To treat other people the way I'd like to be treated. I want to be someone who is steady in their ways."

Angelina watched the emotions roll across Tyler's face. His disbelief. His uncertainty. Followed by something she thought was hope. And then it was all gone. There wasn't a flicker of anything left.

"You don't believe me," she said, her voice flat.

He swallowed and looked at her. "No, I think maybe I do believe you."

He didn't look very certain about it, though, and Angelina blinked back the dampness in her eyes. "I'll prove it to you. Wait and see. I'm a changed person."

"But I'm not," he said.

She could not argue with that. Only God could change the heart of a man. She knew without asking that there would be no more confiding in each other tonight. Tyler picked up his fork and they started to eat their dinner.

Grant me patience, Lord, she prayed silently. *Help Tyler to see he needs to change, too.*

Chapter Nine

Clouds had completely covered the moon and the darkness was deep as Tyler drove Angelina home in his brother's pickup. He could kick himself from one side of this county to the other. He hadn't said enough to please her. Maybe he didn't understand how a belief in God could change her, but he didn't need to make his doubts so obvious that they troubled her.

"I'll see you tomorrow," Tyler assured Angelina as they turned into the Elkton ranch driveway. There were no lights in the main house and just a small one in the bunkhouse. "I'm looking forward to it."

Angelina didn't bother to answer him, and he didn't blame her. He sounded phony to his ear, too.

He pulled the pickup to a stop and turned off the key.

"I meant what I said tonight," he said as they sat there. He had nothing else to offer her. "You're the best friend I've ever had."

Tyler had almost whispered the last. It was a small

thing to offer. And still the words hung between them in uncertainty.

"Am I?" Angelina asked, her voice breaking.

Tyler nodded and gripped the steering wheel with his hands even though they were stopped and there was no need of it.

"So that's it?" she said. "Friends?"

She sounded sad.

"A lot has happened since we knew each other," Tyler said then. "I cannot ask for anything more between us."

"You never have taken me seriously."

"I'm sorry if that's how you feel," Tyler said, running his hand over his head. "I don't mean to be so—" He searched for a word.

"—cold," she offered quietly.

She looked at him then, the yard light shining through the pickup windshield strong enough so they could see each other dimly. They were silent for several minutes and he had the impression she was trying to memorize his face.

"I'm glad we finally got to have a date at least," she said. "Thank you for that."

He nodded as he unlatched his door. Then he stepped out and waited a bit for the pain in his leg to ease before walking around to open the passenger door for her.

"If it was only me," he said, helping Angelina down, "I wouldn't care. But I can't see you hurt. You deserve someone who comes from a healthy family. Someone who knows how to be a good husband and father."

She turned to him then, and put her hand up to lightly

stroke the side of his face. "I know. You've always protected me."

She put her hand down then and he caught it, holding it as they started walking toward the cookhouse. They had not taken many steps before Tyler gave up her hand and put his arm around her shoulders.

"It's a little chilly," he said when she looked up at him.

"Not anymore." She smiled.

A weight lifted off of his heart and they continued walking to her living quarters. The ground was rough and more than once Angelina stumbled slightly. He drew her closer to his side each time.

When they finally stood in front of her door, he bent his head and kissed her softly.

"My feelings are not really cold, you know," he murmured, his lips still close to hers.

She didn't say anything, but her eyes softened.

"I'll see you tomorrow," he promised as he moved back. "For church."

She nodded. "I wonder if my father is even coming tomorrow like he said."

"Don't worry. Either way it'll be fine."

He kissed her once again, and then turned to leave.

He had only taken a few steps when he saw four silhouettes of men standing in the window of the bunkhouse. He waved, getting back an equal number in return.

The partially darkened moon made this a night full of shadows, he thought as he paused a few feet past the bunkhouse to ease the pain in his leg. The yard light didn't give much illumination. And it was quiet. There wasn't even a dog to walk with him, Tyler thought as he made his way to the pickup. Then he stopped and asked himself when he'd become so accustomed to company that he missed it. He prided himself on not needing anyone. He was used to walking alone. He thought that's the way it would always be in his life. He'd never wanted so much as a pet before.

Tyler shook his head at his own thoughts and walked on.

He was still restless as he drove back to his family's ranch. By now the moon was completely covered and, when he looked past the headlights on the deserted gravel road, there was an inky blackness to the sky and land in every direction that made his aloneness feel sharper.

When he first pulled into the long drive that went up to the house, he stopped the pickup in the middle of the road. He could see both of his brother's houses from where he was. They were lit up in the night, the windows making them look warm and inviting. He wondered suddenly how either one of the men had found the courage to leave their solitude and join their lives so permanently to someone else. They had grown up in the same family as him and truthfully, his father's abuse scared him. What if he ended up like Buck Stone? Tyler asked himself that question as he rested his arms on the steering wheel. Children of abusive parents often chose that route themselves. He'd heard that much in the group sessions they had in the home he and Jake had gone to when their mother had been sent to prison.

He would rather never speak to Angelina again than see her suffer like his mother had with his father. Marriage was difficult enough with two people who had some idea of what they were doing. The truth was, if he had to be ruthlessly honest, Angelina would be better off marrying her father's lawyer. The guy sounded stable as a rock. He might be a little clueless when it came to women, but he wouldn't be the first man so afflicted. Angelina could enlighten him. Tyler hoped it was not misguided loyalty to him that was holding her back.

He started the engine up again and continued on to the old ranch house he'd known as a boy. The outside light was on here as well as an overhead bulb in the kitchen. He had expected his mother to be in bed by now but maybe she had waited up for him. The thought pleased him. It had been a long time since anyone had cared about his comings and goings.

When he drove the pickup closer to the house, he rolled down the window and heard Prince barking a welcome.

"Hush, now," he called out the window in a low voice so he didn't wake anyone who might be asleep. He wasn't sure how far the dog's bark would carry, but his mother would certainly hear it if she was in bed.

When Tyler stepped out of the pickup, Prince was there to chase around his feet. Tyler bent down to scratch the mutt behind his ears.

"Doing okay, are you, Prince?" he asked as he straightened up.

Then he looked down at the dog. When the dog wasn't bouncing around, he did have a dignified look to him. "Maybe Angelina knew what she was doing when she named you Prince Charming."

The dog seemed to have no opinion on that so Tyler patted him on his head as a reward for welcoming him home anyway and sent him on his way.

As Tyler walked closer, he saw that someone had brought the round bowls of wildflowers outside and lined them up against the side of the house. They probably needed some sun to continue growing in the black earth packed in those containers. He was touched once again that Angelina had gone to so much trouble over his memorial service.

By the time he reached the back door, he smelled cinnamon. He figured someone had made tea recently so he knocked on the door softly. His mother called for him to come inside.

The single bulb over the table cast the corners of the kitchen into shadows. His mother was sitting down with a cup in front of her. She had a white cotton robe on and her hair swept back with a headband.

He smiled as he remembered. "Is the church still asking women to buy white robes?"

His mother nodded. "They never get enough used robes for the angels in the church pageant."

"And the men still buy brown ones for the shepherds just so they can donate them when they're finished wearing them?"

She smiled as she lifted her cup of tea. "What can I say? It's tradition."

Tyler walked over to the table and sat down across from her. "It's a good tradition. I always wished we could have been part of the nativity show the church did every year in that old barn. I guess it's something to see the angel swing from the rafters. The kids at school would talk about it for weeks after it happened."

"There were a lot of things you boys didn't get to do," his mother said as she set her cup down.

"It wasn't your fault."

Tyler wondered why he hadn't noticed before how much his mother had aged. Maybe it was the harshness of the single light above them, but her cheeks seemed hollow and her eyes troubled.

"It wasn't all your father's fault, either," she added.

Tyler felt a tremble in his hand. "Are you ready to tell me?"

His mother nodded.

She didn't say anything so he cleared his throat. "I thought I knew what it was until tonight."

"You did?" she asked cautiously.

He nodded. "I thought it was because I didn't go inside the barn that day when you two were arguing. I thought if I had the courage to do that, you wouldn't have had to face him alone and everything would have been different."

"Oh, Tyler," she said as she put her hand over his. "I had no idea."

"But Angelina told me you weren't the one to kill him."

She withdrew her hand from where it had lain on top of his and turned slightly away. "No, but I did have a part in it."

She folded her hands in her lap in a schoolgirl pose that seemed to give her some comfort.

"Buck Stone wasn't always the man you knew," she began quietly. "He didn't drink much at all when I first married him. He had some difficulty with the ranch though shortly after that and he said he was drinking to relieve his stress. I didn't think much about it at first. I was busy taking care of my babies. Wade was three years old that year and Jake was past the baby stage. And then one night Calen Gray brought Buck back from some bar in Miles City. Buck had passed out cold. I was scared he was sick and I asked Calen to stay for a while in case we needed to take Buck to the hospital since our pickup was in Miles City still parked outside the bar."

She paused then to catch her breath.

"That's not so bad," Tyler said.

She held up her hand. "I'm not finished. I will never know if I was more worried about Buck being sick or if I just wanted a chance to talk with Calen. But he and I stayed up, spending all night talking. I hadn't seen him for some time. He was a friend from high school and he reminded me of happier times."

His mother stopped again. "And I found him attractive. More attractive than I found your father back then. Oh, we didn't do anything. I was married to Buck, and Calen was his best friend. But the feelings were there."

"Well, you were lonely. Just talking to another man isn't so bad."

"It felt like it was. Your father was suspicious and finally accused me of betraying him that night. I must have looked guilty. He didn't believe me when I said nothing happened. And then when I discovered I was pregnant with you, he came to believe you were Calen's son."

"You never told me."

"Of course not. You were only a boy and had nothing to do with Buck's delusions. I don't know if he said something to Calen or not, but Calen moved away from Dry Creek shortly after you were born, so you never knew him."

"Yes, I did. He taught me how to fish."

"What?"

His mother's eyes looked startled.

"Calen taught me how to fish in the Big Dry Creek. The summer when I was ten. When I said I was going to the coulee to hunt for rattlesnakes, I always took my fishing pole with me. And Calen was there every Sunday afternoon."

"I didn't know he'd come back to the area then. I mean, I know he's here now, but—"

"He said he'd been gone for some years—maybe he came and went."

His mother looked pale, her skin in startling contrast to her black hair. She was rubbing a corner of the wooden table and Tyler knew it wasn't conscious.

"I think he's the one who sent you the wreath," she finally said. "For your funeral."

Tyler sat still for a moment. "But why?"

His mother shook her head. "Maybe he knows you could have been his son if we'd given in to our feelings that night."

The shadows at the edge of the kitchen seemed to grow darker.

"So my father thought I wasn't his," Tyler finally found the words to say. There had been many days in the past when he wished Buck Stone wasn't his father, but finding out that the man thought he wasn't was disorienting.

"All you boys take after me and my Cherokee grandfather," his mother said with a slight smile. "Buck couldn't claim you looked like anyone else."

"And that's why Wade and Stone gave me the best piece of land for my house," he continued, letting the pieces fall into place in his head.

"I expect so," his mother said, her weariness evident. "I had to tell them about this, too, in fairness to their father. I wanted all of you boys to know he didn't start out that way he ended. Jealousy ruined him."

"So Wade and Jake wanted to be sure I knew I was an important person in this family?"

His mother nodded. "They knew your father was always the hardest on you. They wanted to make it better."

All Tyler could do was try to blink back his tears.

All of those years, he had worked to gain his father's approval when he should have been looking to his big brothers instead.

His mother stood up and patted him on the shoulder.

"We'll talk more later if you want," she said. "Right now, I'm tired."

Tyler stood up and opened his arms to his mother.

"Sleep well," he said as he hugged her. "It's good to be home."

She nodded her head as she turned to the living room. She had to walk through there to get to the hall that led to her bedroom.

"I'm going to make a quick phone call," Tyler said. "But I'll keep my voice down so it won't disturb you."

With that, they both walked into the living room. Tyler went to sit on the sofa and his mother went into the hall that led to her bedroom. After he figured she had enough time to get into her bed, Tyler reached for the telephone.

Angelina was brushing her hair and trying not to cry when the phone rang. She was sitting in front of the old framed mirror that hung against the wallpaper in her living area and she could see her eyes were puffy. She loved the cook's quarters here, which consisted of this small room, a bedroom and full bath, but tonight the whole place had seemed too small. She had wandered through the rooms for the past half hour, trying to find some place that felt like her home. For the first time since she left her father's house in Boston, she missed the window seat in her bedroom.

The phone rang again so she stood up and walked over to answer it.

"Hello?"

"Angelina?"

If she had caller ID on this phone, she wouldn't have answered. Since Tyler left a half hour ago, her emotions had been on a roller coaster.

"Yes," she acknowledged, trying not to breathe too deeply because that would release the tears still in her eyes.

"I hope you're not asleep yet."

"There hasn't been time."

There was silence on the phone for a moment.

Then Tyler spoke. "I just wanted to say I enjoyed tonight. And I hope you sleep well."

"I hope the same for you," she whispered.

"I'll see you tomorrow then," Tyler said and then added in a softer tone. "I just wanted to hear your voice."

Angelina's tears stopped with his words. "Me, too."

"Good night now."

"Good night."

Angelina sat there after the phone line had gone dead.

Thank You, Father, for easing my heart, she prayed. *And if there is any way... Well, you know my feelings. I trust You with them.*

Chapter Ten

A Sunday in July wasn't the best time to visit a church in this part of Montana, Tyler thought as he gave the white building an assessing look, all the while feeling the sun on his face. There were no shade trees close to the structure and the pitched roof had dark shingles that would absorb the heat. He didn't see an air-conditioning unit, either, and in a building that old he doubted they had more than ceiling fans. It was going to be miserably hot inside.

But it couldn't be helped, Tyler thought as he turned to offer his mother a hand as she stepped down from his pickup. She was wearing a lilac cotton dress. He'd already needed to reassure her that he wasn't upset about her revelations of the night before so he had no choice but to look as cheerful as he could.

He wasn't ready for a church though. His assumptions had been shifting around so much lately that he didn't know what he thought about a lot of things anymore. He knew he should find a reason not to go inside the church building, but nothing compelling came to him and he didn't want to disappoint his mother.

"Careful," he said as she started walking. The ground was nothing but dirt and tended to have tire tracks left from the drying of the last rain.

Tyler limped along behind her. The cement steps leading up to the church were already warm and the underside of the metal handrails would be scorching before long. The door at the top of the steps was open so Tyler figured that confirmed there was no air-conditioning inside.

Still he followed his mother and soon stood in the front hall of the church. He'd been this far the one time he'd gone to Mrs. Hargrove's Sunday school class so he knew that the door to his left led down some narrow stairs to the basement. The wide archway in front of him led to the main church area. Along the opposite wall was a long wooden coatrack with a bench beneath it. A stray red mitten hung from one of the hooks. It had probably been there for months. Tyler supposed the rack was used in winter, but at this time of year no one wore anything that needed hanging.

His mother had walked straight toward the main part of the church and then turned back to look at him when it was obvious he wasn't following.

"You go on," he said. "I'm going to look at the bulletin board over there."

His mother nodded and he felt obligated to go over to the corkboard so he wasn't a liar. He didn't care what was pinned to the thing, but he wasn't quite ready to go inside the real part of the church. He thought he had figured out God years ago, but he didn't know now.

What he couldn't make sense of was the way his family had changed. He had seen the courage his mother had shown last night. He'd watched the determination in her eyes as she accepted her part in what happened years ago with his father. He knew many people would have kept silent about their failure and let the other person take the whole blame. But she respected the truth enough to tell him. When he had time later to think more about her revelation, he figured it would change some things inside him to finally know why his father didn't like him.

He glanced over his shoulder and saw a young couple with a child follow his mother into the room.

When Tyler turned back, he saw a photo of himself. It was tacked under a banner that said Pray for Our Troops. He remembered when Angelina had snapped that picture of him. The two of them had been sitting on a wall by the school steps, waiting for a friend of hers to meet them. It had been an ordinary day.

As he looked at the picture, another couple walked behind him. He turned around then. He might as well go in and sit down. He was more nervous about being here than he had been as a boy. He still felt like he was an intruder, waiting to be found out. If he thought about it at all, he knew he'd almost welcome someone asking him to leave.

It was quiet when he stepped into the main part of the church. He didn't want to linger in the aisle of the church so he quickly spotted his mother and walked over to the pew where she sat. The polished oak felt smooth on his hands as he sat down beside her. Then he felt air moving and looked upward to where two large ceiling fans were slowly making circles to give people some relief from the heat.

He'd barely adjusted to the pew when Wade and Amy came and sat on the other side of his mother. Then an older woman who he didn't recognize walked to the organ and began to play softly.

So far, Tyler told himself a few minutes later, church had been all right. The closed blinds gave a golden hue to everything and no one was staring at him. In addition, the song being played on the organ was very uplifting. He relaxed and told himself he shouldn't have been so worried. He heard a few whispers and rustles as more people came inside, but there was nothing he couldn't handle.

He saw no reason why he couldn't come here and spend a peaceful hour on a Sunday morning. It would make Angelina and his mother both happy. He settled back into the pew, confident he had everything under control.

And then Pastor Curtis got up and walked behind a wooden stand. The first thing the man did was ask everyone to bow their heads and pray together. Tyler was relieved no one expected to hold his hand this time. He wondered if that tingling he'd felt had been static from him touching someone else.

After the prayer and a few songs, the pastor read a

story from the Bible and it didn't make any sense to him. It was about a group of men who carried a crippled man to Jesus, lowered him down through the roof of some house and let him lie there in front of everyone, all of his weakness exposed and him dependent on a stranger to heal him.

Tyler hoped he never had any friends like that. They should have left the man where he lay until he could help himself. Struggle built character. Showing weakness in front of others did not.

Impatient with the whole thing, Tyler turned his head around, thinking there must be a clock on the back wall. Instead of a clock, he saw Angelina sitting in the back row on the other side. She glanced over at him and their eyes met. Then she glanced down and he turned around. It was enough to soothe his restlessness, though. She was here.

Angelina had gotten here late and she had a tiny spot of maple syrup on the white blouse she now wore with her gray skirt. It was down by her waistline and barely visible, but it showed how agitated she had been this morning. While she had been making pancakes for the ranch hands, she'd gotten a call from Mrs. Stevenson, her father's secretary, to say they had arrived at the Billings airport and were renting a car to drive to Dry Creek. During the night, Angelina had somehow forgotten her father had said he was coming here.

She suspected the reason her mind had let it go during the night was because her father never showed up when he said he would in her life. He'd promise to be at birthday party after birthday party and he never came. Sometimes Mrs. Stevenson would rush in at the last minute with a big present that was supposed to be from him, but Angelina knew he hadn't picked it out. On a couple of occasions, he looked at her blankly when she thanked him so she figured it had been his secretary who had arranged everything. Angelina could not fault her memory if it assumed this visit would be like all of the others.

But she'd found out earlier this morning that something was different this time. Apparently if her father became annoyed enough with her, he seemed willing to keep his word and actually come to see her.

That wasn't Mrs. Stevenson's fault though and Angelina had tried to keep her voice pleasant for the secretary when she called. The woman said she couldn't talk more than a minute because they were ready to leave the airport, but she assured Angelina they would be to Dry Creek as soon as possible. She'd told Mrs. Stevenson she'd be in church this morning and they could meet her there. Until then, Angelina intended to carry on like nothing extraordinary was happening today.

When Pastor Curtis gave a page number for the final hymn, she couldn't help but notice how relieved she felt, though. She told herself it was the heat, but it was also her nerves.

She never had thought her father would come to Dry Creek. She loved the place, but he would think it was beneath her. It would be too small, too poor, too insignificant for him. What if all her newfound friends took a dislike to her when they saw the disdain he would have for them?

She wished suddenly that she hadn't mentioned anything about meeting at the church. Maybe she should drive her convertible to the edge of Dry Creek and stop her father's vehicle before he met anyone else. Yes, she decided that was the best plan as everyone stood and the pastor gave the final prayer.

The aisles were filled with people and it seemed like everyone wanted to say something to her this morning. Most of them were thanking her for the work she'd done on Tyler's memorial service or asking her for the recipe for her stuffed mushrooms. She looked across the church and saw people were clustered around Tyler and his mother, too.

One of the things she'd liked about Dry Creek was that everyone was so friendly, but today she kept her remarks as brief as possible and tried to work her way to the door. The longer she thought about it, the more she decided she should keep her father away from her new friends here as much as possible. And, he certainly wouldn't stay long when he realized she wasn't going to be swayed by his arguments so it shouldn't be too difficult to isolate him. He might even leave before he met anyone else.

She had just shaken Mrs. Hargrove's hand and was almost to the door when she heard a commotion outside.

"Put your hands up and step away from that door." Sheriff Wall's bullhorn sounded from outside.

"What in the world?" Mrs. Hargrove asked in astonishment.

The whole church went silent.

A couple of the men went over to the windows and lifted the blinds slightly.

"The sheriff has a gun aimed at some people by a limo," one of them said.

"Limo?" Angelina repeated in dismay.

She looked across the church and saw Tyler staring at her. They both knew what was wrong.

"I'm sure everything's fine," Tyler said then, his voice holding enough authority to keep everyone in their place. "I'll go check it out."

"But you don't have a gun," one of the other men reminded him.

"I won't need one," Tyler said.

His brother Wade spoke up from some place close then. "Well, at least get that knife of yours out. The one for rattlesnakes. I know you have that much with you. On second thought, you better wait for me."

Tyler didn't seem to be listening, though. He was already most of the way to the door. He stopped when he got to Angelina.

"Don't worry. You know it's some misunderstanding," he said to her quickly, his voice low so no one else would hear.

She wanted to tell him not to go out there, but he was gone before she opened her mouth.

And then he was opening the door.

Wade was right behind him, muttering something about a fool when he passed Angelina.

"Keep your hands where I can see them." The bull-horn sounded again.

Lord, have mercy, Angelina muttered, her worry turning to prayer as she headed for the door, too. It had to be her father out there. What in the world had he done wrong?

Chapter Eleven

Tyler looked out from the church steps and he saw what he dreaded.

Sheriff Carl Wall indeed had his gun aimed at Mr. Brighton and his small group. Tyler did a quick study of the people. He recognized Angelina's father and Mrs. Stevenson. And a man he had only seen in a photo Mrs. Stevenson had shown him—that man was Derrick, Angelina's lawyer soon-to-be fiancé.

"Easy now," Tyler called out low and casual as he put his own hands in the air just so no one could mistake his intent as he slowly walked down the church steps.

He sensed someone at his side and looked over to see Wade scowling at him.

"Put your hands up," Tyler said softly to his brother. "And don't make any sudden moves. We don't want to make the situation worse."

Wade grunted. "Okay, baby brother."

Then, to Tyler's relief, Wade did as he asked.

"This is Tyler Stone," he called out then, a little

louder so he could be sure Sheriff Wall heard him. "We're coming over. There's nothing to worry about. My brother Wade is walking beside me so, if you hear two of us, that's who we are."

Tyler kept walking forward as he talked. No one generally shot someone if they were talking to them. At least, he hoped not.

"I'm sorry to say I know these people," Tyler continued. He was halfway across the street to where the sheriff had his standoff.

At the sound of Tyler's voice, everyone in the Brighton group looked over at him.

"Everybody stay steady," Tyler called out, willing them all to do just that because as he'd gotten closer he'd noticed a flash in the sun that led him to believe Derrick might be armed. As he took a step closer, he could see the man held something in his hand.

"Drop the knife, Derrick," Tyler said, taking another step closer. "Everyone will breathe a lot easier if you do."

"What about Wild Bill Hickcock over there?" Derrick jerked his head at the sheriff. "He's armed."

"He's the law," Tyler said, trying to be patient.

"It's just a pocketknife," Derrick said.

"It's still a lethal weapon." Tyler wondered what kind of law the man practiced. Then Tyler remembered it was finance. Probably not much need to know weapon laws there.

"We weren't intending any harm," Derrick protested, but he did let the knife fall to the ground so Tyler let him have his say. "It's hotter than blazes out here and Mr. Brighton needs water. It was a medical emergency and we thought the door to the café might just be stuck."

Tyler wondered if the lawyer thought that excuse would work in a court of law.

Apparently, he didn't because he added, "Besides, we haven't had any breakfast."

"That doesn't give you the right to break into a business," the sheriff said firmly. He relaxed his stance and didn't look as inclined to shoot as he had earlier though. "If you wanted a drink of water, you could have come over to the church."

"The café is closed on Sundays," Tyler added. "The sign's up and everything."

"Well, that's no way to run a business," Mr. Brighton finally spoke. His face was a little red and he was breathing fast. "A man like me would leave a good tip for something to eat on a day like today."

"The owner goes to church on Sunday," Tyler said. By now he and Wade were close enough to the sheriff to be part of the group. "I don't think she cares how much you'd tip."

The sheriff finally put his gun back in his holster and looked at Tyler. "Who are they anyway?"

"Angelina's father and his—" Tyler searched for a word that would cover the group "—his staff."

Derrick grunted, but didn't protest the description.

"They are from back east," Tyler said, trying to think of some defense.

"The laws there are the same as they are here," the sheriff noted, not yielding.

"But they're city folk," Tyler added. "Nothing ever closes back there."

The sheriff grunted at that, but didn't say anything more.

He did turn around so he was facing Tyler, though.

"What do you think I should do with them?" the sheriff asked.

Tyler shrugged. "Hard as it is to believe, they didn't mean any harm. Did they ruin the lock?"

The sheriff nodded toward Derrick. "That one had his knife out working at the door when I spotted him. I don't know if the others could see what he was doing or not. I figured they were all in the getaway car so I made them all step out."

"You thought we meant to rob this place?" Mr. Brighton burst out in astonishment. "Why my watch alone is worth more than the whole thing!"

With that, Angelina's father held up his wrist to show the gold watch he wore.

Tyler didn't bother to debate the issue, but he was pretty sure that old guitar hanging on the wall inside the small café would buy a dozen or so watches like that. It was a collector's item.

"Mind if I hold that watch," the sheriff said then, as he stepped over to the older man. "I'll just keep it for security until you pay for the damages your party caused on that door."

"I've never heard of anything like this," Mr. Brighton

sputtered then, his face getting redder than it already was in the heat. "Don't you know who I am?"

"You're Angie's father," the sheriff answered. "Real nice girl you've got. And it's on account of her that I'm going to ask the shop owner if she wants to press charges before I decide whether to run you off to jail."

"Jail?" Derrick grew a little pale at that.

Angelina's father finally took the watch off his wrist and handed it to the sheriff. The lawman then took it over to his patrol car and opened the trunk. Tyler figured the sheriff needed to tag the watch somehow. But, when the sheriff came back he had three bottles of water in his hand. They were dripping and looked cold to Tyler.

"Compliments of Custer County," the sheriff said as he handed out the water to the three. "I keep a cooler in the trunk on days like this. This sun can kill a man if he doesn't drink some water."

"Thanks," each of the three said to the sheriff, their tones varying.

Mrs. Stevenson was graciously pleased. Derrick seemed a little surly, but he took the bottle nonetheless.

By this time, more people had come out of the church. Tyler could hear them behind him as they walked over toward the café. They should be scolded for coming out to a scene like this until they got the all-clear from the sheriff. But he had to admit it was comforting to have them at his back.

He turned around then and saw that the first person coming was Angelina.

Even in all that had happened today, she looked crisp

in the heat, her blond hair put up in some kind of a swirl and her white blouse setting off her tan.

"Father?" Angelina whispered when she got close enough to speak. Her blue eyes snapped with dismay.

Tyler didn't envy her father. Not the way she was looking at him as if she couldn't believe what he'd done. He took a step closer to her. He supposed it was instinctive. He'd never let her walk into trouble alone yet.

Angelina sensed someone next to her and looked up briefly to see Tyler there. His brown eyes were steady as they met hers and she took comfort in his relaxed stance.

"I have never been so embarrassed in my life," she said to Tyler, her voice low. "And you know that is saying something. How could my father do something like this?"

"I think he was hungry," Tyler offered, his voice mild.

Angelina turned her eyes back to her father.

"The limo ran out of pretzels," he agreed as though that explained it all. "And there wasn't any place to get breakfast once we left Billings. I even stopped at the edge of town here at that gas station. It was closed, too. And the vending machine only had chewing gum in it. No one can make a meal out of chewing gum."

By that time, Angelina was aware of someone else standing close. She looked over and saw Linda, the owner of the café. The woman was looking puzzled.

"I'm so sorry," Angelina said to her. "My father is

completely out of line and if you want to lock him up, be my guest."

"Angelina!" her father protested in disbelief.

She turned on him then. "Well, it's time you learned that just because you have all the money in the world, it doesn't mean you get to do what you always want. You have to have some respect for other people. You need to show up when you say you will. You need to—"

She felt Tyler's hand on her elbow so she stopped. He was right. She didn't want to have this conversation with her father in front of the whole town of Dry Creek.

It was silent for a moment.

"I don't want to cause trouble with your father," Linda finally interjected. "I'd say if he pays for the repair of the door, we're okay."

"That's kind of you," Angelina turned to Linda and said. "I'll see you're paid."

"I can pay for it," her father said, his voice tight.

Angelina knew she had offended him. His face was red. He wasn't used to anyone talking back to him.

"Well, whichever," Linda said now, her voice filled with the kind of forced cheer people use when they want the situation to just get better. "You both know where to find me."

By then almost the whole congregation of the church was out in the middle of the street, wondering what was going on and whispering about the people in the limo.

Angelina wanted to go crawl under a rock and hide.

She saw Gracie Stone come up beside her and walk

a couple of steps closer to Angelina's father than anyone had so far.

"I'd be pleased if you and your friends would come to my home for Sunday dinner," Gracie said, just as calm as anyone could be. "I have some spaghetti sauce simmering in a Crock-Pot and you're more than welcome to share it with us."

After she fixed breakfast, Angelina had Sundays off at the bunkhouse. She usually left a platter of cold cuts and potato salad so the ranch hands could help themselves when they were hungry.

"We couldn't impose," her father said stiffly and Angelina realized she had wounded his pride.

"It's all right," Angelina said then and walked over to her father. She stood on her tiptoes and gave him a kiss on the cheek. His skin felt hotter than even the sun would have caused.

She needed to talk to him about trying to control her life. But she didn't need to do it right now. He needed to get inside and rest somewhere.

She looked around at the staff her father had with him. They all looked tired and a little scared.

"This wasn't the welcome I wanted you to have," she said to them with a smile.

"Please, do come to dinner," Gracie added, this time her voice sounding less formal. Then she looked up at Angelina. "And, of course, I'm counting on you coming, too."

Angelina's eyes looked over at Tyler.

He grinned. "My mother made two apple pies yesterday. She's a good cook and they're just waiting there for us."

"Don't tell the Elkton cowboys your mother bakes pies," Angelina said to Tyler in a stage whisper and got the grin she was hoping to receive.

"I'll drive you back later today to get your car if you want to come with us," he said.

Angelina nodded. "Thank you."

"Well, if my daughter is going, then my staff and I would be most pleased to take you up on your kind offer," her father said to Gracie.

"Well, I guess that's all settled then," Sheriff Wall said, turning to go back to his car.

Angelina's father then walked over to Linda and stood in front of her, reaching into the pocket of his suit jacket and pulling out a long thin wallet. He peeled off a handful of bills and gave them to the café owner.

Linda looked at them. "These are all hundreds." She spread them out in her hand. "Way too many. There has to be fifteen, sixteen hundred dollars there. One would probably be enough to get the lock repaired."

"Keep them," Mr. Brighton gestured. "I don't want anyone to think I don't pay for my mistakes."

Angelina flushed. "I only meant you need to be responsible," she said.

"Well, let's be going then," Gracie finally said with a smile to them all. "You can follow my son's pickup out to our ranch. His is the black one with the Indian chief's head on the back bumper."

"We know the pickup," Angelina's father growled. "It sat in my garage for years."

"And I thank you for it," Tyler said then, putting one arm around his mother and a hand on Angelina's back. "I must say I'm hungry, too, though, so we might as well get driving out to the ranch."

Then he looked down at Angelina and asked, "You okay?"

She nodded in relief. Soon, with some more prayer, she would be ready to sit down and discuss matters with her father. Until then, they could all use something to eat. She only hoped her father didn't stir things up anymore.

Chapter Twelve

Ten minutes later, Tyler, Gracie and Angelina were climbing up the steps to the back door of the Stone family house. Angelina took a deep breath. The smell of spaghetti sauce greeted them as they walked through the enclosed porch. The kitchen windows were closed, but the white curtains still fluttered, reminding her of springtime.

She saw why the curtains were moving when she went inside the house. A tall rotating fan sat on the far side of the room and moved the air around.

"It's cooler than I expected in here," Angelina said as she walked over to the row of hooks behind the door. "Mind if I borrow an apron?"

"Help yourself," Gracie said, and then pointed up at the ceiling. "The secret to cooler air is up there. The hot air gets trapped in the second story and that keeps it pleasant down here. Then at night we just open the bedroom windows up there and the temperature goes down quickly."

"I've been sleeping like a baby," Tyler said as he stood in the middle of the kitchen before looking at his mother. "Now, where do you keep the leaves for this table?"

"They're in the hall closet," Gracie said as she walked over to the refrigerator. "And we'll need all of them. There will be eleven of us with Wade and Jake and their families."

"What would you like me to do?" Angelina asked as she finished tying the apron around her waist.

"Check to see if your father's limo is almost here," Gracie said as she opened the refrigerator door. "They were following us close enough to be coming down the drive by now."

Angelina walked over to the kitchen window above the sink. It had a clear view of the lane coming into the ranch house. "I don't see them."

"Well, they'll be here soon," Gracie said. "I don't think they could miss the turn into the ranch here."

"If they don't show up soon, I'll go out looking for them," Tyler said as he came back with three extension leaves for the table. "I'll take a damp cloth to these meanwhile."

Gracie lifted some containers out of the refrigerator. "We have enough of your appetizers left to serve them before dinner." Then she turned to look at Angelina. "I'm sure your father would love to taste them. He must be so proud of you."

Angelina laughed at that. "I don't think cooking for

people ranks very high on my father's list of important things to do with one's life."

Gracie stood up then, a plastic box in her hands. "He might change his mind after today. Where would the world be if no one ever cooked?"

Angelina knew that, if her father wasn't so hungry, he would likely leave here without trying any of her cooking. He might not even realize what it meant to her. It took Angelina a moment to understand, but then she knew her father wasn't the only one to blame. She'd never told him that some things were important to her. Maybe if she had said something, he would have done things differently.

Humbled by that realization, Angelina set to work. She wasn't going to let that happen today. She took the stuffed mushrooms out of the container and lined them up on a baking sheet. On Friday night, she hadn't baked all of the mushrooms so the ones she served tonight should be as fresh as the first ones. The mini quiches would reheat well so she put them on a smaller metal sheet. She even had enough raw carrots and green pepper slices to make a plate of those.

She planned to not just serve these appetizers, but to tell her father as best as she could that cooking like this was something she put a lot of effort into and she wanted his opinion. It might just be a temporary job in her life, but she did want his blessing on her work.

Once she finished putting the appetizers in Gracie's oven, Angelina turned her efforts toward the table. Tyler had washed the extension leaves and needed help to pull the two ends of the round table apart so the leaves could be added.

"It's been a few years," Tyler said as he nodded for Angelina to pull on her half.

Gracie came back into the kitchen through the living room with an ivory lace tablecloth. "We haven't had this much company in a long time so I thought we could use this. It's only been used a few times when the Mitchells came over to dinner during the holidays."

Tyler and Angelina finished expanding the table and Tyler had spread the tablecloth over it.

The water was boiling on the stove for the spaghetti noodles and Gracie had brought out lettuce and tomatoes to make a salad.

Suddenly, there was a horn sounding outside in fast little beeps.

"What's that about?" Gracie asked as she turned away from the tomatoes. She only had them partially diced.

Tyler went to the door and opened it to look into the yard.

"It's the limo," he said in surprise. "It sounds like something's happened."

Tyler quickly walked out the door, taking huge steps all the way to where the vehicle stood with its side door open.

"I don't suppose they've had a flat tire?" Gracie said as she walked over to the door where Angelina stood.

"The tires look fine to me."

Angelina told herself there was no reason to worry.

Derrick must just be the kind of guy who liked to call attention to himself. But, somehow, that didn't seem right.

Then she saw the side door on the limo come open. Derrick had climbed out of the driver's seat and was hurrying around the front of the limo to get to that door. Mrs. Stevenson climbed out and then leaned back inside.

"Something's wrong," Angelina whispered to Gracie and then started to run toward the limo.

Please, please, please, she prayed, not even able to tell God her sudden worry. If anything happened to her father, she didn't know what she would do.

Tyler crawled through the limo door behind Derrick. Mr. Brighton was stretched out on the long seat on one side of the vehicle. His face was flushed and he looked disoriented. Tyler noticed then that a blood pressure cuff was lying on the seat opposite the one that held the older man.

"Has he been having trouble?" Tyler asked quietly as he moved along behind Derrick until they were both close to Mr. Brighton.

Derrick looked back at him, worry clear on his face. "Why do you think I was so determined to get him water and something to eat back there? The heat and those pretzels were a bad combination."

"So it was an emergency," Tyler said, regret filling him that he hadn't paid more attention to the flush on the older man's face. "You should have said something— I mean, I know you did, but you should have said he was sick."

"He made us promise not to let Angelina know." Derrick put his hand on the older man's forehead. "He doesn't want her to worry."

Derrick loosened the collar of Mr. Brighton's shirt and reached under the seat to bring up a small pillow that he slid under the man's head.

"You obviously know what you're doing." Tyler watched the practiced way Derrick's hands moved.

"I was a medic in the service," Derrick said, reaching over to take the other man's pulse.

Tyler nodded. It wasn't often that he misjudged someone, but he had here.

"Can you help me get him into the house?" Derrick asked then, looking at Tyler. "He'll be more comfortable in there."

Mr. Brighton stirred where he lay and then whispered, "Angelina."

"We won't say anything to her," Derrick assured the man and then gave Tyler a warning look. "Will we?"

"It would be best if her father told her," Tyler said. If the lawyer noticed the lack of a promise, he didn't comment.

Derrick gave the older man some more of the water the sheriff had given them and then declared they were ready to move Mr. Brighton.

"If he leans on both of us, he'll be able to walk in," Derrick said. "He just needs to go slow."

Mr. Brighton did look better, Tyler thought as he backed out of the limo to give Derrick room to position the older man to exit.

Mrs. Stevenson had been just outside the door and stepped closer to Tyler. "How is he?"

"Improving a little, I think," Tyler said as he looked down at the woman who had been a faithful secretary to Mr. Brighton for years. Her brown hair, short and curled, had some gray in it now. Her green eyes had always been expressive. She dressed quietly and always seemed to fade into the background.

She nodded in relief.

"You could have told me, you know," Tyler said to her gently. "I would have worked harder to convince Angelina to go home."

"He didn't want her to know," the woman said. "And I couldn't take the chance that she would find out once you knew." She smiled then. "The two of you were always close."

"There never was a wedding, was there?" Tyler asked.

"Oh, yes." She looked at him in surprise. "Or there could have been one. Derrick has always wanted to date Angelina. I thought you knew that."

Derrick came out of the door then, and Mr. Brighton followed after him.

Tyler stood to the older man's right and Derrick took the left side. Sometimes, Tyler thought, a man didn't get to choose the ones he needed to stand beside.

The muscles in Tyler's shoulders ached from the pressure the ill man put on them, trying to balance himself so he could make the short walk to the house. Tyler's left side might be his injured one, but he didn't mind the discomfort. He was glad he was here to help his old boss when the man needed him.

Angelina stood on the top of the porch steps, tears in her eyes.

"He's okay," Derrick said as they walked the older man forward.

Tyler was amazed at how convincing the lawyer sounded.

"Just a little heatstroke," Derrick continued as he shot a warning look to Tyler.

Tyler nodded back at him. Now was not the time for anyone to tell Angelina what was going on with her father. Once they were inside the house, he could only hope the older man decided to tell his daughter himself what was wrong.

Each step seemed to take an eternity, but it was only fifteen minutes before they reached the house.

"You can take him back to my bedroom," Tyler's mother said as she pointed through the living room to the small hall that led there. "He'll be more comfortable lying down. I took the fan back so the air will be cooler by the time you get him there."

Derrick and Tyler both nodded.

"Once you get me settled." Angelina's father paused to catch his breath. "Go ahead and eat."

"I'll sit with you," Angelina declared. "I don't know how you can think I could eat at a time like this."

That seemed to please Mr. Brighton, but he said, "You need your strength."

Tyler and the two other men started to walk again,

passing through the darkened living room before they came to his mother's bedroom. A blue sheet had been thrown over the quilt on top of the bed and they walked Mr. Brighton over there and helped him lie down.

"I'll go get you something to drink," Tyler said after the older man was settled.

"There's no need," Angelina said from the doorway.

Tyler turned around to see her entering with a glass of water and a plate with some crackers on it. He wanted to protect her from the hurt she would experience when she learned her father was seriously ill. But for now, all he could do was stay close.

Angelina balanced the plate in her hand as she carefully stepped forward and put the glass of water down on a coaster on Gracie's nightstand.

Then she looked down at her father.

"I didn't know what you'd like, but I thought this seemed bland enough," she said. His face was pale in places and flushed in others. "You look like you might have the flu or something, too."

He shook his head and his color did improve. "I'm fine. I just need to rest a bit."

She looked up at Tyler and Derrick then. Both men were standing close by as though they expected someone to need them. "Thanks for bringing my father in here."

They both nodded.

"I can sit with him, though," she continued. "There's no need for the two of you to miss out on dinner. Wade and Jake and their families are here now and everything is ready to eat. Gracie just took the garlic bread out of the oven."

"I don't think I should leave," Tyler said, crossing his arms.

"I'll call if we need anything," Angelina insisted.

"You're sure?" Tyler asked.

She nodded.

Then she looked back at her father. The truth was, she'd like to be alone with him for a bit. She'd been scared when she'd seen how frail he was getting out of that limo. As much as she had chaffed recently, thinking he was trying to control her, she had a wellspring of love for him. He was her daddy. He had done his best to give her a good home after her mother died. She had never thought about how hard it must have been for him to lose his wife to cancer and then have to care for a daughter who was a toddler. He'd given his life for her.

She looked up and saw that both Tyler and Derrick had gone, although someone had left the bedroom door open so they'd hear if she called even with the noise of the fan.

"You should be the one getting married," Angelina said softly as she walked over to the wall and brought back a wooden chair. "I don't know why you think I need to be the one to use those church reservations you made."

Her father smiled at that. "I don't think marriage is in my future."

"Why not?" Angelina said as she sat down and took

her father's hand. "You're young. You're handsome. And don't forget rich. You'd make a good catch for some woman."

Her father chuckled. "Those were the qualities I had on my list for your husband."

"I know," she said with a grin. "Mrs. Stevenson showed me the list."

"That woman—" Her father sputtered. "She has no business—"

"She cares," Angelina interrupted. "And you know it."

Her father quieted at that.

"In fact," Angelina said, deciding to give voice to a long-held suspicion, "I think Mrs. Stevenson would go out with you if you asked. Her husband has been gone for a long time now. I know the two of you have always been fond of each other. A widow and a widower. That works. And you have a lot in common. Why—"

Her father raised a hand to stop her flow of words.

"It's too late for that now," he said, and she thought he sounded sad.

Angelina would have stopped at the expression on his face anyway. Something wasn't right.

A few minutes later, her father spoke again.

"I'm leaving Mrs. Stevenson a bequest in my will," he said then. "Derrick knows about it and I wanted you to know, too. It's fairly large and I didn't want anyone to think she had suggested it to me or anything like that. In fact, I haven't even told her about it for fear she'd refuse it outright."

Angelina nodded, but was silent.

"I want you to see that she takes the money," her father said then, and looked at her with an expression she'd never seen in his eyes before. He desperately wanted her help.

"I'll be sure she takes the money," Angelina promised softly as she put her hand out to caress his cheek. "And I'll let her know it is a gift of your love."

He nodded and closed his eyes. "It'll be a comfort to her when I'm gone. You always were so much better with emotional things than I was."

"She loves you, too." Angelina bent down to kiss her father on the forehead. "We both do."

He rested then, with her sitting beside him watching the movement of his chest as he breathed in and out. The sound of the fan spinning kept her company as a trickle of tears ran down her cheek. Her father had never spoken about his will before. In fact, he'd never said much of anything with the hollowness in his eyes that she had just seen. He believed he was dying.

About that time, she heard a footstep and looked up. Tyler was standing in the doorway.

"I thought you might like me to sit with him while you get something to eat," he said as he walked over to the bed. "He looks like he's sleeping."

She stood up and turned to him.

"I— He—" She tried to say the words and couldn't. Tyler must have understood though because he opened his arms and she stepped into his embrace.

"I think he's dying," she whispered as he held her.

His arms tightened around her at that and she knew it was true. She wept then, and he rocked her slightly where they stood.

Four hours later, her father was settled in the limo and Prince was, too. Angelina had put her dog on a leash and stowed him away in an old chicken crate Gracie had found out in the barn. Derrick said there would be room for him in the small plane if Angelina didn't take any luggage.

She was going back to Boston with her father. She had called Calen at the bunkhouse and explained the situation. He assured her the ranch hands wouldn't starve. If need be, he said, he'd pay Linda from the café to bring out hamburgers every day for the noon meal and they could have scrambled eggs for supper. It wouldn't be long until the regular cook was back anyway since her mother was doing better.

"Those cowboys will be more worried about you than their stomachs anyway," the ranch foreman assured her. "Which is saying something. They care about you."

"I care about them, too."

Angelina handed the keys to her convertible to Tyler then. "I left it by the church. Just bring it over here and park it anywhere. It should be fine if you keep the tarp on it."

He took the keys, but didn't say anything.

She turned to Gracie then. "I don't have much left in the cook's quarters over at the Elkton place. So if you could put it in the two suitcases in the closet there, it will all fit in the convertible's trunk. Everything will be fine there."

Gracie nodded. "I'm happy to do anything to help."

Angelina looked around the kitchen then, committing to memory the way the curtains fluttered at the window when it was open and the red bird that had been so nicely painted on the wall by the refrigerator. Gracie wordlessly walked back into the living room and left her alone with Tyler.

"I need to go," she whispered as she stepped close enough to touch him on the cheek.

"I know," he said as he reached up and covered her hand with his own. He brought her hand around until he could kiss the palm of her hand. He curled her fingers around that kiss. "Something to remind you of me."

She blinked back the tears.

"Boston is only a plane trip away. I can send you a ticket."

He shook his head at that. "A man needs to pay his own way."

They just stood there and looked at each other then as the minutes slowly moved by on the wall clock.

"If my father wasn't so sick," she said finally.

"I know," Tyler said and opened his arms to her.

She went into his arms again, but this time he didn't let her stay for long.

"Everyone's waiting," he reminded her, as he stepped back a little.

She nodded and tried to smile. "Call me."

"You'll do fine," he said as he started to walk toward the door. "Take care of your father."

With that, she walked out the door into the afternoon sunshine. She noticed that the heat had lifted a little and gray clouds were coming in from the west. She expected they would have a thunderstorm tonight.

As the limo pulled away from the Stone family ranch, Angelina kept her eyes on the house, watching it grow smaller and smaller in the distance. Then she looked over and saw her father was watching her with concern on his face so she smiled for his benefit.

"I hope that dog of yours likes Boston," her father said gruffly then.

"He'll be fine," she assured him. They would both be just fine.

She turned to look back again even though she could no longer see the stone house. She felt tears in her eyes and blinked them away. She had to put her own feelings aside. Her father needed her.

Chapter Thirteen

Eight days had passed since Angelina left to go back with her father and Tyler had spent the days repairing the roof on the barn. He'd had to go slowly because his left arm still could not function as it should and it took a fair amount of balance to move around on the pitched roof.

But he hadn't quit until he finished the job.

After eating a quick supper with his mother, he limped into the living room where he sat down, figuring he would keep himself company until the room went dark as the sun slowly set. There was no television here and, while the light from the kitchen came in if he opened the door, it wasn't strong enough for reading. Besides, he found it restful to just sit in the shadows and stare at the gravestone he and his brothers had managed to push into a far corner of the room.

He heard a sound and looked up to see Wade opening the door. Then he walked over and sat down on the sofa next to Tyler.

"So, what impossible thing did you do today, baby brother?"

Wade stretched his legs out in front like he had all the time in the world.

"Don't call me that," Tyler protested mildly. "And, for your information, it's not a crime to put in a full day's labor."

"I suppose not," Wade answered easily as he looked around the room. "Is there some reason you don't have any lights on in here?"

"I'm enjoying the sunset. It filters in through the curtains."

"The sun set an hour ago."

"Oh."

They were both silent for a minute.

Finally, Wade cleared his throat. "Mom is worried about you. Says all you do is sit in here at night and stare at your gravestone like someone who's just waiting to die."

"There's no law against a man sitting and thinking."

"I suppose not," Wade said, his uncertainty clear. "But maybe you could help me out here. What are you thinking about?"

"I'm not thinking about dying when I look at it. I'm thinking about the line that says 'Tyler Stone—beloved son, brother and friend.'"

Wade didn't say anything, but he'd turned to Tyler with an intensity that was clear even in the darkness.

"I've never been beloved before," Tyler said softly. "I'm just thinking about what that might be like."

"Oh," Wade said and then paused. "I see the problem now."

Tyler shifted himself on the sofa. "I don't know that—"

"It makes perfect sense," Wade continued.

Tyler waited for his brother to go on, but he didn't.

"Well, are you going to tell me or not?" he finally snapped.

"It's our father," Wade answered, his words slow and deliberate. "Buck Stone left his mark on you. All those things you used to do—tracking down rattlesnakes, chasing that bull when he was ten times your size and we all knew he could turn on you. That about gave me a heart attack. But, don't you see—you did everything you could think of to make Buck respect you. Thinking then that he'd love you and accept you."

Tyler started to protest, but he knew the words were true so he finally closed his mouth.

"You're still doing it," Wade said. "Taking on the hardest, most dangerous jobs and not giving up when any rational person would."

"You should talk. You rode prize-winning broncos in the rodeo. People die doing that."

"That's why I know, baby brother. That's why I know. All three of us boys had the same problem. We never could earn our father's love, but we sure tried."

"Well, at least, he liked you and Jake. I always knew that."

Tyler realized he wasn't ready for this conversation so he started to get up. "No use pretending otherwise."

Wade grabbed hold of his arm and didn't let him go.

"I'm not planning to pretend with you," Wade said. "But I want you to hear me out."

Tyler sat back down.

"It's not trusting other people that's troubling you," Wade said. "It's letting them love you without you earning it that's the problem."

"A man should stand on his own two feet."

Wade shook his head. "Sometimes you just can't do it alone. God doesn't count how many dangerous things you do or don't do. Brave men and cowards. We all need His help and He loves us all the same. You don't have to be a hero for Him to notice you."

"I don't see how—" Tyler started and then stopped because Wade had stood up and gone into the kitchen.

Wade returned carrying their mother's Bible. "It's all in here."

His brother walked over to turn the lamp on and then sat back down beside him. "Now I'm going to show you a thing or two that our mother learned in prison."

"Could you start with the guy who was lowered through the roof?" Tyler asked. "The one the pastor talked about on Sunday."

Wade nodded as he started turning pages. "That story got to you, did it?"

"I just don't know how a man can ask others to help him like that," Tyler admitted.

"That's the heart of the whole thing," Wade said as he looked up from the Bible. "No man can do it alone.

All of us need God. And not just to go to heaven. We need Him more here on earth."

"God and I haven't been on the best of terms," Tyler admitted.

"But you can be," Wade assured him as he looked down at the Bible again. "Here. I'll show you how."

An hour later, Tyler felt hope rise up inside of him so strong that he couldn't keep quiet.

"Are you sure about all this?" he asked his brother for the third time.

Wade nodded. "As sure as I am of anything."

"Then I want to be a Christian. Right now. Tonight. I had no idea."

Wade grinned at that. "Let me read to you how it's done."

With that, he opened to the Gospel of John.

The next morning, Tyler woke up and smiled. He had one more dangerous thing to do before he settled into life on his family's ranch. And, in the spirit of brotherhood that he'd shared with Wade last night, he was going to let the other man help him as much as he wanted.

Tyler didn't even wait for breakfast. He started walking across the field at dawn and, by the time he reached Wade's house, a light was on in the kitchen. Tyler knocked and was let in.

Wade's kitchen was all white and chrome with Danish blue plates hanging on the walls. Coffee was brewing on the counter.

"Something wrong?" Wade asked. His hair was not combed and his T-shirt not tucked into his jeans.

Tyler shook his head. "I could just use some help, that's all."

"Really?" Wade beamed. "So you came to your big brother?"

Tyler nodded. "My final check from the military is tied up. It's a good amount since it covers those months when I was dead. I think that's why they're having so much red tape. But anyway—"

"How much do you need?" Wade interrupted as he looked over at the counter. "I have a checkbook in the drawer there. Unless you need cash?"

"I can cash a check when I get to Billings," Tyler said. "If you could make it for three hundred dollars. I have some money with me, of course, but I'm not sure what the flight will cost and I might need to spend a night in Billings if I can't buy my ticket the same day I travel."

"You're going to Boston, aren't you?" Wade asked, grinning. "To see Angelina?"

Tyler nodded. "I realized she took Prince with her."

"You're going to get the dog?" Wade's grin faded. "I know you like the animal, but I'm not sure that—I mean, it is her dog."

"No." Tyler shook his head. "That's not it. I realized I never expected her to even remember the dog was hers. In high school, she would have left without giving Prince a second thought. If she took the dog, she has changed. And now God has changed me, too. Maybe I could be a better husband than I've always thought."

Wade's grin was tentative this time. "So, it's a good thing?"

Tyler nodded. "A very good thing."

"In that case, tell Angelina we miss her around here."

Wade walked over to the cabinets in the kitchen and opened a drawer. He took out a checkbook. "I'm going to make it for a thousand dollars just because you never know when you're traveling."

"I should be able to pay you back in a week or two."

"You'll do it when you can," Wade said. "I'm not worried."

With that, Wade pulled out a pen and wrote a check. "How's Angelina's father with his cancer?"

"Mrs. Stevenson says he's holding his own. The doctor doesn't expect him to live more than a few months but they're doing everything they can for him."

"You're still calling her every morning," Wade said, handing him the check.

Tyler nodded and folded the check. "It felt good to pray with her on the phone when I called earlier. They're two hours ahead of us so she was at her desk. She's worried about Mr. Brighton, too."

Tyler put the check in his shirt pocket. "Thanks."

Then he reached out a hand to his brother.

"Mrs. Stevenson knows you're coming?" Wade asked as he shook hands.

Tyler nodded. "I told her I would be there today or tomorrow, depending on how soon I can get a flight."

"God be with you, baby brother," Wade said.

"I'm counting on it."

* * *

Almost two thousand miles away, Angelina stepped off the elevator into the Brighton Security offices with a large white box in her arms. Her blond hair was pulled back into a severe bun and she wore a black suit with no jewelry. She had insisted on doing something useful with her time and her father had asked her to help Mrs. Stevenson catch up with the filing. Angelina agreed as that put her in a good position to watch over her father in his corner office.

"This came to the house yesterday while I was at work." Angelina walked over and rested the box against the woman's desk. "I don't know what to do with my father. I've told him and told him there was no need to get that wedding dress for me. And now this, he bought two bridesmaid dresses."

Angelina opened the box and a satin lavender dress lay on top with a deep rose dress in the same material lying under it.

"My favorite color," Mrs. Stevenson said with a smile as she reached over to touch the lavender one. "But don't worry. Your father is only trying to give you the wedding of your dreams."

"Ever since we got back here, he's been ordering things. Although, I guess if it makes him happy, he can buy a hundred dresses," Angelina said.

She looked down the long hallway that had offices opening off of it. Her father had sold off most of his businesses in the last month, saying he wanted to spend his remaining time with family. It was bittersweet knowing he'd waited so long to do so.

"How do you think he looks this morning?" Angelina leaned down and whispered.

"He's holding his own," Mrs. Stevenson replied in a low voice.

"I can hear you out there," a booming voice came from her father's office, the one that was all of the way at the end of the hallway.

"Nothing wrong with his hearing," Mrs. Stevenson said with a smile.

"I best go in and say good morning." Angelina stood up straight and adjusted her suit so the line of buttons in the front was right where it should be.

"I have a feeling it's going to be a most interesting day," Mrs. Stevenson said mysteriously.

Angelina looked over at the woman in horror. "He hasn't ordered anything else, has he? I already got the embossed napkins with my name and *groom* on them. If I ever do get married, I think I'd want the man's name on there, too, and not just the word 'groom' like I picked him off a sale shelf somewhere."

"Just look at them as samples," the older woman advised calmly.

"He ordered a thousand of them," Angelina protested. "They came two days ago. Along with a big box of wedding fortune cookies and another of paper plates." Angelina paused. "Actually, the paper plates aren't so bad. They have gold trim to match the napkins, but they don't have any names on them—just a pair of golden doves flying off together into the sunset."

"Well, see," Mrs. Stevenson said in an encouraging voice, "you like some of the stuff."

"I thought I might send the paper plates to the guys in the bunkhouse. They can use them for their sandwich plates on Sunday when the cook is off. No one would have to do dishes then."

"I heard that," her father said again. This time his voice didn't carry as well, though.

"He needs to be drinking more fluids," Angelina said as she hurried down to his office.

Angelina knew she worried over him all day, but sometimes even that didn't seem enough. The doctor said her father needed to rest more than he did and to watch his stress. She made it her mission to see that he did. She had missed out on so much with him; she wanted to capture every minute they had left.

He, on the other hand, seemed determined to spend his remaining days planning her wedding.

When she got to his office, he had a brochure of floral arrangements on his desk.

"What's your favorite flower?" he looked up at her and asked sheepishly. "A good father would know that, wouldn't he?"

Angelina walked over and kissed him on the cheek. "Wildflowers. And you're a good father."

"Finally," he said.

"In God's time," she replied and kissed him again. She wished she had not waited so long to be at peace with her father. She'd wasted so much time pushing him away for what he hadn't done that she hadn't accepted the love he did have to offer. Losing her mother had made it difficult for her to accept love from anyone. She knew that now. If she didn't let anyone close, she would not risk losing them.

She didn't want to continue like that. She wanted to love and be loved.

Chapter Fourteen

Tyler ran his finger around the collar of his shirt as he stepped into the elevator going up to the Brighton Security offices. Unfortunately, it didn't help his shirt much. He had ended up changing planes in Washington, D.C. and sleeping half of the night in the airport. He'd taken a taxi from the airport, but now that he'd caught a glimpse of himself in the mirrored elevator, he was wondering if he shouldn't have stopped first to change. However, this was his best shirt and was probably no more wrinkled than the one in the duffle he still carried.

The elevator doors opened just then and he saw Mrs. Stevenson.

"You're late," the woman said as she walked toward him. "I was expecting you yesterday after your call."

"I got here as soon as I could," Tyler said as he gave a quick glance around.

"Angelina isn't in yet this morning," Mrs. Stevenson said with a little smile. "She'll be here any minute, though, if you want to wait."

"Is that Tyler Stone out there?" A voice boomed from the end of the hall. "Send him back here."

Mrs. Stevenson shook her head and whispered. "He never used to yell like that from his office."

"Maybe time feels too short now not to ask for what he wants." Tyler lifted his duffle. "Mind if I leave this by your desk?"

"Go right ahead."

Tyler had only been in Mr. Brighton's office a few times. Usually they had staff meetings in the conference room.

"Well, don't just stand there," the older man said when Tyler got to the doorway. "I've been expecting you."

Large glass windows, looking out to the harbor, made up two walls in the corner. Beige chairs were scattered around and Mr. Brighton sat behind a huge mahogany desk.

"I came to turn in my paperwork." Tyler walked inside.

"Hmm." The older man looked at him. "How tall are you again?"

"I beg your pardon." Tyler stood there wondering if the man was having a reaction to some kind of medicine.

"I'd guess six foot—"

"Close enough."

Mr. Brighton nodded. "Come over here and sit down so we can talk."

Tyler sat in the chair opposite the older man's desk.

"Glad you came," the man said then. "I've been thinking about that bonus I owe you."

"You don't owe me a bonus. I quit. Remember?"

Mr. Brighton shrugged. "Still, I owe you."

Tyler realized they could go on all day, back and forth on that point. He wasn't sure his courage would hold that long.

"I came here about Angelina," he finally said.

"I knew it!"

Tyler couldn't afford to quit before he said his piece. "I figure I owe you notice that I plan to ask her to marry me."

Tyler kept looking squarely at Mr. Brighton. He wasn't expecting the man's face to grow pale and his eyes to grow damp.

"I have no reason to think she'll say yes, though," Tyler added hastily. Maybe he shouldn't have said anything with the other man's health being what it was. "Don't distress yourself."

"I used to say you didn't have what she needed."

"You used to say I was too poor to take care of her," Tyler said with a smile. "And you were right. Still are, in fact. I've just realized I can't let money stop me from asking her."

Just then Tyler heard Angelina's voice greeting Mrs. Stevenson.

"Come on in here, Angelina," her father said in a voice loud enough to be heard on the floor below. Fortunately, Brighton Security had that floor too so there would be no complaints.

Tyler felt his heart start to beat faster.

It almost stopped altogether when he saw her. Angelina stood framed in the doorway, the smile on her face fading from what he could only assume was shock at seeing him.

"Tyler," she said and seemed unable to go further.

"Come on in," Mr. Brighton said, gesturing to his daughter. "The boy here has something to ask you."

Tyler had faced enemy fire before, but it had never been like this.

"I thought dinner—" Tyler started to stutter as he looked to the older man for a reprieve.

"Nonsense. We don't have time for that."

Tyler stood up and walked closer to Angelina. She was looking at him now like she was almost afraid of what he was going to say.

Tyler looked down the hall behind Angelina and saw Mrs. Stevenson standing there watching, too.

"Father," Tyler prayed, not realizing he was whispering the words aloud. "If I ever needed help, now's a good time."

He saw Angelina's eyes brighten. "You're a Christian?"

Tyler nodded and cleared his throat. "I tried to write out some words on the plane ride here, but I have the paper in my duffle out by Mrs. Stevenson's desk." He took a deep breath. "What I want to ask is this—will you marry me? I've loved you since I first met you and I expect to love you until I die. But I'll understand if you think it's not something you want to do. I mean—I don't have the kind of money—"

"Yes." Angelina interrupted him.

He looked at her not sure he'd understood her.

"Yes, yes, yes—I'll marry you," Angelina repeated. "I love you, too."

That was answer enough for Tyler. He stepped forward and kissed her.

Angelina was the first one of them to hear the applause. She looked up from Tyler's embrace to see her father stop clapping long enough to reach under his desk and set a big garment box on top.

"I guessed right," her father said in triumph to someone behind her and Angelina looked around to see Mrs. Stevenson walking toward them. "He's six foot all right."

Then her father opened the box.

"Tyler," Angelina whispered so he would turn and see.

Her father held up a black tuxedo that had to be Italian. On the lapel, in a thread that was even darker, someone had stitched a motif of an Indian chief in full headdress.

Angelina still had her hand on Tyler's arm and she felt the shock run through him.

"It should fit you, son," the older man said. "I'll admit I wanted my daughter married so she'd be taken care of when I leave this world, but I should have made more of an effort to see she will be happy, too. You'll see to that just fine. We had your waist and shoulder measurements in your file for some reason, but we'd neglected to get your height."

"For me?" Tyler stammered. "I thought—"

"I'll admit I've been shortsighted in the past," Mr. Brighton said. "Probably still would if I hadn't heard my daughter pouring her heart out to that dog of hers."

"Prince?" Tyler whispered as he drew her back into his arms.

"He's a good dog," Angelina said. "Understanding, too."

"I'd say he's a very good dog," Tyler agreed as he bent down and kissed her again. This time there was no applause. Just the sound of soft footsteps as her father and his secretary left the room.

"I plan to be a good husband to you," Tyler whispered as he held her. "I didn't think I could, but I've been watching Wade and Jake. They didn't follow our father's footsteps with their families. There's no need for me to follow him, either, especially now that I have God to guide me."

Angelina looked up at him. "And if you do have a problem, we'll talk it out and pray about it." She hesitated, remembering how she had kept her father away by seeing only what he couldn't do. "I promise to let you be imperfect, too, so you can feel free to tell me when something's wrong."

Tyler leaned back a little. "You're sure about that?"

She grinned and nodded. "You'll always be my hero, but I want us to be close enough to share everything."

Tyler smiled. "My mother would agree with you on that one—sharing the good and the bad,"

Then he bent down and kissed her.

Angelina sighed and then whispered, "I particularly like sharing the good."

Tyler chuckled. "Me, too."

So he kissed her again.

Epilogue

"It fits perfectly," Angelina said as she stood in front of the mirror in Gracie Stone's bedroom. The adjustments her father had ordered on the wedding dress made it one she would cherish forever. The white satin skirt flowed out like the petals of a flower and the soft netting that rested on the billowing skirt gave it a princess look. Even the touch of European lace that her father had asked for at the neckline pleased her.

"Mine is perfect, too," her friend Kelly Norton said as she smoothed down the skirt of the rose bridesmaid dress. Kelly had squealed in delight when Angelina told her she was marrying Tyler.

"What I don't understand is why your father thought to include me," Mrs. Stevenson said from where she stood in the doorway to the bedroom. "Or how he knew I loved lavender."

Angelina smiled at the older woman. "You've always been part of our family. I hope you know that."

No one had told Mrs. Stevenson about the inheritance

she was going to receive, but Angelina suspected this day might mean more to the woman anyway.

Mrs. Stevenson blinked back tears and then smiled. "It's time for us to go. They're waiting."

The three of them picked up Prince as they passed the porch on the way out to the field behind the lilac bushes. The dog had lavender-and-rose-colored ribbons in a bow around its neck. Prince seemed to understand it was an important day and not one for barking.

As they walked, Angelina looked over to the house that she and Tyler were having built. Her father had insisted on paying for the house as his wedding present to them, but he had agreed with her and Tyler that the rest of the money in the Brighton family could safely be put in a trust for any children she and Tyler might have someday.

Tyler had worried about the house not being grand enough for her until she assured him that the only things she really wanted were a window seat in a quiet spot of the living room and a deck large enough for them to go out at night and look at the stars.

After they passed the lilac bushes, Angelina saw the wildflowers. Her father had sent in a specialist to seed this field and encourage the flowers to grow. There were bluebells, morning glories and violets. All of them stood brightly in the green grass. A white tent had been set up and a hundred and fifty folding chairs placed in rows.

The town of Dry Creek had come to the wedding and she smiled widely at her friends before looking up at the ones who mattered most to her. Her father stood beside Tyler along with his brother Wade. Pastor Curtis was next to them with Gracie Stone's Bible in his hands.

When Angelina finished walking up the aisle between the chairs, her father stepped forward and gave her away with the traditional words.

She leaned up and kissed his cheek after he did and Tyler reached across to shake her father's hand. Her father was going to spend as much time with them as his health would permit after they got back from their honeymoon. When he needed to be in Boston, she and Tyler would be with him there.

After giving her away, her father stepped back into his best man role and the pastor continued with the ceremony. When they said their vows, both Angelina and Tyler put their hands on his mother's Bible. They had talked about it and they wanted that gesture to symbolize the importance that book was going to have in their lives. Gracie Stone's struggles had made them stronger already.

"And, now," Pastor Curtis said and then paused for effect, "I pronounce you husband and wife."

The pastor turned to Tyler. "You may now kiss your bride."

Angelina didn't even hear the applause as Tyler dipped his head to hers in a powerful kiss that promised a lifetime of love.

* * * * *

Dear Reader,

First, thank you for coming back to Dry Creek with me. I am truly enjoying writing the stories of each of the members of the Stone family in my RETURN TO DRY CREEK series. As always when I write these books, I think of you and hope you will be pleased to read them when I'm done.

This book is about Tyler Stone, the youngest member of the family. Tyler was the one who was most apart from his mother and brothers. It seems that many families have one child who, either willingly or through other circumstances, stands apart from the family. In writing this book, I did not go into all of the ramifications of that kind of an action, but I do want to acknowledge that it happens more often than any of us would like. If you have someone in your family that you are estranged from, I would encourage you to do all you can to reconcile with them.

Next up in the series will be *Second Chance in Dry Creek,* Gracie's story. I am already writing about her chance at a new life.

If you have some time, drop me a line and let me know if you are enjoying the series. I love to hear from readers. Just go to my website, www.janettronstad.com, and email me there.

Sincerely yours,

Janet Tronstad

Questions for Discussion

1. Tyler Stone was reluctant to go back to Dry Creek because he felt the small town had betrayed him and his family. Have you ever been disappointed in a group of people? Did you try to work things through with them? What advice on this would you give to others? Do you have any insights from the Bible?

2. Tyler makes the statement that he didn't write to his mother much because he didn't know what to say to her when she was in prison. The Bible asks us to visit people in prison. Have you ever done so? How was it?

3. A character in the book, Mrs. Hargrove, did write to Tyler's mother when she was in prison. How do you think Mrs. Hargrove felt about doing this? A kindness to others can often bring a blessing back to us.

4. What did you think of Angelina's relationship with her father? If you could suggest any Bible verse to her, which one would it be?

5. Just before the book began, Angelina Brighton adopted a stray dog. It seems she did this so she would have someone to be part of her family. Angelina's mother died when she was young and

her father is distant. What other things could she do to obtain this family feeling?

6. Many of us enjoy good relationships with our pets. The Bible talks about taking care of our pets in Genesis 9 when it says "They (meaning all animals, birds and fish) are given into your hand." What do you think this means?

7. Which of the Stone brothers most clearly resembles the prodigal son? Why? Which of the Stone brothers is most like you? Why?

8. The Stone family talks about not having a gravestone for Buck Stone, mostly because they do not know what to say on the gravestone. What do you think they should say?

9. What lessons on life did you learn from this book? Forgiveness? Hope for the future?

10. Tyler is surprised that Angelina liked the small town of Dry Creek so much because it was different than the rich life she lived elsewhere. Were you surprised? Why or why not? Do you think people who have lots of money have happier lives?

REQUEST YOUR FREE BOOKS!

2 FREE INSPIRATIONAL NOVELS
PLUS 2
FREE
MYSTERY GIFTS

Love Inspired

LIREG11B

Love Inspired.

TEXAS TWINS

Follow the adventures of two sets of twins who are torn apart by family secrets and learn to find their way home.

Her Surprise Sister by Marta Perry
July 2012

Mirror Image Bride by Barbara McMahon
August 2012

Carbon Copy Cowboy by Arlene James
September 2012

Look-Alike Lawman by Glynna Kaye
October 2012

The Soldier's Newfound Family
by Kathryn Springer
November 2012

Reunited for the Holidays
by Jillian Hart
December 2012

*Available wherever
books are sold.*

www.LoveInspiredBooks.com

LICONT0812